D0892653

The Beast on the Broch

John K. Fulton

pokey
hat

First published in 2016 by Pokey Hat

Pokey Hat is an imprint of Cranachan Publishing Limited

Copyright © John K. Fulton 2016

www.johnkfulton.com

@johnkfulton

ISBN: 978-1-911279-03-7

Cover illustration by Dawn Treacher

www.dawntreacher.com

The diagram in Chapter Three is based on
illustrations taken from the Historic Scotland site
www.pictishstones.org.uk and is used under the terms of the
Open Government Licence for Crown Copyright material.
Map of Scotland Outline © Can Stock Photo Inc. / rbiedermann

www.cranachanpublishing.co.uk

cranachan

In memory of my dad, Robert, who brought me up with a love of books, and taught me never to let the facts get in the way of a good story.

For my mum Elizabeth and brother Alan, for love and support.

And for Sandra, for everything.

Contents

CHAPTER ONE

On the Broch

I WATCHED THE CORACLE FROM HIGH ON THE BROCH as the little boat made its way up the coast. I was enjoying the way it bobbed along the grey swell with three small figures crowded into it. It was a comical sight—the coracle obviously wasn't meant to hold three, and they'd been bumping and elbowing each other as they tried to row the little boat. My grin faded as I realised—too late—what they were up to.

The little coracle was heading right for my fishing nets.

The shoreline was some way off, but I could see the coracle clearly from my vantage point on the broch. I'd only climbed the ancient ruined tower to pass the time while I waited for the tide to recede a little bit—I'd planned to pull in my nets on my way back to my mother. We didn't have much food left in the house, and a nice fat sea trout would have done nicely for supper.

'Hoy!' I shouted.

1

The boys in the distant coracle showed no sign that they'd heard me. They shipped their single oar and drifted to a halt near my nets. I could see the bladder float bobbing on the sea right next to them. One of the three—a lanky boy, his red hair bright in the last of the sun—leaned out of the coracle and pulled at the net. They were a long way off, but my net looked like it was heavy with fish.

'Get away from my nets!' I shouted, my voice shrill with anger. They were stealing my fish!

They couldn't hear me. They were far too far away. The broch had a good view of the sea on all sides of the peninsula, but because it was right in the middle of the point, it wasn't particularly close to the coastline. I swore, with words I wouldn't dare use in front of my mother.

I stared into the distance. The silvery-skinned fish tumbled from the net into the bottom of their coracle, then the lanky boy started rolling up my net. My net! Not content to steal my fish, he was taking my net, too. I'd spent the long dark winter evenings weaving that net, squinting in the firelight, huddled in a sheepskin, my fingers numb from the cold and blistered from tying the knots.

'Thieves!' I shouted, but still they ignored me. In frustration I picked a loose stone from the top of the wall and threw it in the direction of the coracle. I knew I couldn't reach them. It was too far for me to throw. Even my father couldn't have thrown it far enough. I watched the stone drop into the spiny gorse bushes as the coracle turned inland and the boys rowed towards the rocky beach—where my *other* net was.

I reached for another stone.

A noise of sharp claws scrabbling on crumbled stone came from behind me. I turned quickly, nearly losing my footing on the broch's edge, and my heart stopped. Barely an arm's-length from me, a long-snouted animal stared at me from huge sea-grey eyes. I swayed in surprise, felt my feet slip on the stones, and before I knew what was happening I was falling from the broch.

Long curved claws grabbed at my wrist, cutting into the skin, and I felt my shoulder jerk as it took all of my weight. My feet dangled above the rocks and fallen stonework that speckled the base of the broch. If I fell, I'd break my legs—if I was lucky. I looked up and all I could see was the creature's head silhouetted against the bright sky, the only visible feature a pair of grey eyes, their black pupils slitted like a cat. My feet scrabbled at the wall, trying to get a grip.

The monster started to pull me up towards him, and

I became aware of the teeth glinting in his long snout. I writhed in his grasp.

He growled, a low rumbling more like a wildcat than anything else, and I stopped struggling. What choice did I have? Drop to the jagged rocks below, or let the beast pull me up onto the top of the broch, where I might at least have a chance?

The long curved claws tightened on my wrist, and slowly the beast drew me back up onto the top of the broch wall. I lay on my belly, not sure whether to be more scared by the drop behind me or the beast in front of me.

His long snout twisted into a snarl that showed a row of sharp, triangular teeth. Shark's teeth, I thought, then wished I hadn't. I let out a breath slowly and managed not to whimper.

I pulled my legs underneath me, sat back, and looked at the beast, breathing slowly to calm my racing heart while I tried to work out what I was going to do next.

The beast looked like a cross between a wolf and a dolphin, with short grey-black fur like a seal. He smelled of the sea, too, salty and slightly fishy. His long, narrow snout was lined with pointed teeth, and his huge sea-grey slitted eyes stared at me, unblinking and round. The eyes were so mesmerising that I almost didn't notice the two long horns curving out from his forehead and extending down his back. He stood on four heavily-muscled legs, each ending in black claws. It looked like the beast walked on his knuckles, with the claws curved underneath. A thin tail with a tuft of longer fur on the end flicked at a cloud of midges harrying his rump.

I had never seen anything like him in my life.

Or had I?

'You're... I mean, you look like the stone beast,' I said.

He cocked his head as if he were listening. It almost looked like he understood me.

I rambled on. My mother always said that I talked too much when I was nervous. But I've always talked to animals. If you can keep your voice calm, it's amazing how much they can pick up from your tone. 'Do you know the stone beast? It's the animal on the clan stone in the village,' I said. 'Our clan sign is the crescent, the sword, the snake, and the beast.'

The beast's grey eyes narrowed, and I wondered if I'd angered him.

'Not that I'm saying you're a beast!' I said. 'Of course not. It's just that you look a bit like the beast on the stone.' I edged backwards, hoping I wasn't making any sudden movements that might cause him to attack.

The low growl came from the beast's throat again. The growl that sounded an awful lot like a warning.

There was no way I'd make it down the broch if he attacked me. It was a dangerous old ruin, six times the height of a tall man. It had thick double walls made of closely-fitting dry stones, with a central courtyard open to the sky. If you wanted to climb up or down, you had to use the crumbling stairs inside the double walls. If I tried to make it down the inside of the broch, he'd be on top of me in a second.

The beast took a half-step towards me, his jaws parted enough to show the glint of sharp, sharp teeth, and I braced myself.

I'd have to jump.

Chapter Two
Home Without Supper

THE BEAST TOOK A STEP TOWARDS ME, then paused, lifted his long nose to the air, and sniffed. He growled, then, with a scattering of loose stones, he turned and leapt from the broch, landing with a loud thump on all four legs. He hit the ground far below me and set off at a run into the gorse bushes. Within seconds his grey hide blended with the long evening shadows and he disappeared from sight.

'Hoy! Talorca! Is that you up there?' came a shout from the opposite side of the broch. I scrambled over to the edge and looked down. It was Aidan, the little nuisance who followed me around like a puppy. He was a couple of years younger than me, and for some reason he'd decided that because he had no brothers and sisters, and neither did I, he'd attach himself to me like a limpet. He looked up at me, scratching his armpit idly. 'Your mother won't be happy you've been climbing the broch again. I'll tell.'

The beast must have heard—or smelled—Aidan coming.

I'd never been so glad to see the stinky little trouble-maker. 'Just wait there, Aidan,' I called. 'I'm coming down now.'

At the bottom, Aidan said, 'You're in trouble.'

I ignored him and strode off towards the beach. If I hurried, I thought I might still be able to catch the thieves before they made off with my other net.

'Where are you going?' asked Aidan. 'What's happening?' He ran alongside me.

I made a face that I hoped he didn't see.

'Did you see that coracle in the firth, Aidan?' I asked, trying to distract him from my trouble-making. He was an awful nuisance, but if you pushed one thing into his head, another popped out to make room for it. With any luck he'd forget to tell my mother about me climbing the broch. I didn't want to tell Aidan about the strange beast, though. For one thing, I wasn't entirely sure what I'd seen, and I didn't want Aidan running off and telling everyone that I was imagining things.

'Eh?' said Aidan. 'No, I didn't see anything.'

'There were some boys stealing my nets,' I said.

'I bet that was the Dalriadans from across the firth.'

'Dalriadans? But why would... There they are!' The boys had brought their coracle close in to the rocky beach, and were pulling in my net—the one that usually contained nice fat crabs, and sometimes even the odd lobster. I raced across the sharp rocks, feet splashing in the rock-pools, throwing off my cloak as I ran, leaving Aidan open-mouthed in my wake.

I grabbed at the net, but the tall boy, the one with the bright red hair, had taken a strong grip, and was bracing his legs against the side of his little boat.

'Get off my net!'

The boy shouted something gibberish in reply, and tugged hard. I could see the snapping black pincers of a lobster sticking through the holes in the net, nipping at my fingers. I pulled back, and the three boys laughed at me.

'It's mine, you thieves!' I wrapped the net around my hand for a better grip, but the tall boy was too strong, and with a tug he pulled me off the rock. I lost my grip, and before I could catch myself I fell face first into the sea.

With a splutter I broke the surface, blinking the water from my eyes. I got to my feet—the water was barely up to my waist—but it was too late. As I pulled off heavy strands of black bladderwrack seaweed that had got tangled up in my hair, the boys were rowing their coracle back down the coast, my nets with their catch in the bottom of their boat, the sounds of their laughter echoing across the water.

'Thanks for your help,' I said to Aidan as I picked up my cloak from where I'd dropped it and tried to dry myself off as best I could.

He shrugged, then wandered off to find someone else to annoy, leaving me to make my way home.

Our house was built by my father with his own hands, and it was the best in the village—except maybe the Old Woman's house. But that was only right. The Old Woman was in charge of the village, and had many responsibilities, so it was only fair that we gave her the biggest house. The rumours were that my mother would be the next Old Woman, which would mean that we'd have to leave our own cosy house, and move into the big house right in the centre of the village. I wasn't looking forward to leaving my home—the only place I'd ever lived in—so I tried not to think about it. Anyway, I thought, with a bit of luck, it would be years before that happened. The Old Woman was tough as stone. She'd be around for ages yet.

Our house was built with a solid oak frame bound tightly with strips of cowhide, dry stones carefully selected, neatly shaped, and skilfully fitted together to form the round walls. Over the oak beams was a roof of turf that kept the heat in. We had a heavy cowhide over the doorway that I had weighted with river stones sewn into the bottom edge to stop it blowing about in the wind. It wasn't a small house, either. There was plenty of room for sleeping and cooking and food storage, and even space for two or three animals in a separate partition when it got really cold. In the coldest winters we were glad of the extra warmth our few long-haired cows provided—even if we weren't so happy about the smell. It was a comfortable home, even in the long winters when the north wind sent sleet and hail—the doorway faced south-east to catch the morning sun and to turn its back on the coldest winds.

'I'm back,' I called out as I pulled the door covering aside, breathing in the peat-smoke smell of home.

'What happened to you?' asked my mother, seeing my bedraggled appearance. She was pushing a bone needle through a heavy woollen tunic—she always liked to get started on the winter clothes in plenty of time. The dim orange flickering of the low fire in the central hearth gave her just about enough light to see by, but she could stitch clothes with her eyes shut.

'I fell into the sea.'

My mother showed no surprise, as if falling into the sea

11

was something I did every day. 'And where's the catch?'

'Sorry,' I said, showing my empty hands.

'Oh, Talorca,' said my mother. 'I only asked you to do one thing.'

'It's not my fault,' I protested.

'It never is,' said my mother with a sigh. 'What would your father have said?'

I flinched. My mother only ever brought up my father when she was feeling miserable and spoiling for a fight.

'No, it's really *not* my fault this time,' I said. 'The nets are gone. Some boys in a coracle stole them—and the fish, too. Aidan thinks they were Dalriadans.'

'Don't be stupid. Why would Dalriadans be stealing nets around here?'

'Aidan thinks...'

'Aidan! When does Aidan ever think? He does a lot of talking, but not much thinking. You shouldn't listen to that daft boy.'

I shrugged. There was no point in arguing when my mother was in a mood like that. Mother didn't like Aidan very much. She wasn't actually wrong about him—he didn't do an awful lot of thinking—but for some reason she thought that was enough to treat him with contempt, while I thought he was funny. In small doses. When he wasn't following me around like a chick that had lost its mother.

'We'll have to have plain oat cakes,' said my mother. 'A bit of fish would have gone nicely with them, but I suppose it can't be helped.' I don't think she believed my story.

'Anyway,' I said, recognising the signs of an argument waiting to begin. I had too much filling my head, what with the beast on the broch and the stolen nets, to waste my attention on arguing with my mother. 'Whoever took them, the nets are gone, so there's no fish.' I always complained about making nets—I hated it—so maybe she'd believe my story if I started making a replacement. 'Do we still have some of that twine? I should get back to making another net.'

My mother glared at me, her dark green eyes over high cheekbones making her look like an angry wildcat. I met her gaze. 'Over in the corner, next to the box of needles,' answered my mother. She bent her head over her stitching, her long hair—still rich and dark without a hint of grey—falling over her face.

I picked up my bone netting needle—the one my father had made for me—and started knotting the twine to add to a net I'd started and abandoned a while back. I was glad of something to keep my fingers busy while my mind

13

worked. Now I was back in the familiar environment of my home, my encounter on the broch with the beast seemed strange and dream-like. Had I imagined it?

No, of course not. I could remember the way the breeze rippled his short fur, the warm sea-smell that came from him. I rubbed my wrist. I still had three red marks where his claws had gripped me.

'Mother,' I began.

'Yes?'

'You know our clan stone?'

'Of course,' she said.

'What does it mean?' I asked.

'Mean? It doesn't mean anything. It's the symbol of our clan. Crescent, sword, snake, beast.'

'It has to mean *something*,' I said.

'Your father's clan symbol was the salmon and the double-disc,' said my mother. 'That doesn't mean anything. It's only a symbol.'

'But father's clan were salmon-fishers, weren't they?' I'd never thought about clan stones as having an actual meaning before, but if the beast was a real beast, was there a reason it was on our stone?

My mother sighed. 'Yes. I suppose so. But we're not beast hunters, are we? Or snake hunters. The people who hunt

14

snakes and beasts under the crescent moon.' She shook her head.

'What *is* the beast?' I asked.

'I *told* you,' said my mother, 'it's only a symbol. An imaginary beast. I've never seen an animal like it. Have you?'

'Of course not,' I said quickly. I bent my head over my net and concentrated on tying knots. 'That would be ridiculous.'

CHAPTER THREE
The Stone Beast

THE NEXT MORNING, I SAT OUTSIDE OUR HOME, my fingers making knotting motions even though I'd left my unfinished net inside. When I closed my eyes I could see the net in front of me—in my mind's eye I completed another knot with my netting needle and started another loop.

I blinked the image away and got to my feet. At least when my mind was filled with knots, it wasn't filled with anger at the Dalriadan thieves, and wasn't bursting with questions about the strange beast on the broch. Normally in the morning I'd be picking a spot to put my net out, but until I finished making it—and it would probably be several days before I managed to complete a net big enough—I was at a loose end.

I wandered into the centre of the village. The peaty smell of cooking-fires hung over the roundhouses, and my stomach rumbled. I'd had only oat cakes again for my morning meal. If it was going to be a while before we had any more fish, I'd have to take a look at the vegetables growing in our plot of land and see if any were ready to harvest. Even a few crisp leaves would make the oat cakes go down a bit more easily.

We had some cows, and some geese, but slaughtering any of them too early was a recipe for starvation once winter came. That was how we lived our entire lives—in preparation for the next winter.

Maybe I'd take a trip to the shore to gather some shellfish. That would be better than nothing.

I found myself standing right in the centre of the village, in front of the clan stone. It was a massive rectangular slab, slightly taller than me and half as wide as it was tall. On one side, facing the monastery, was engraved a circled cross with detailed knot-work. I knew that the cross was old, but not as old as the design on the other side—the Old Woman had told me that the stone was put up when the monastery was built. I walked around the cross to look at the other side. This side showed a much more ancient design. The Old Woman had said that a rough boulder had stood on this site for hundreds of years before the monastery came, and it had been carved with the same design that had now been copied onto the cross-slab. At the top was a crescent, turned so that its horns faced downward, marked with

17

curled patterns and a snapped arrow design in a V-shape. Next was a strange two-bladed sword, of a type I'd never seen, then a snake with a broken Z-shaped spear.

At the bottom was the beast.

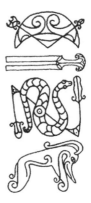

There was no mistaking it. The stone showed the beast in profile, with its long horns stretching along its back, its long snout and huge round eye, and tight curls where its feet would be. It was a strange way to depict those curved claws that I'd seen—there was no hint on the stone of just how sharp and cruel they'd looked in reality. I rubbed my wrist where the claws had left an imprint.

Someone in our clan, in the long-distant past, had seen a beast. A monster. And had drawn this symbol, and adopted it as the sign of our clan. What did that mean? If my father's clan used the salmon on their clan-stone to show that they were salmon-fishers, had my mother's ancestors been beasts-hunters? Friends of beasts?

I didn't like the idea of us being beast-hunters.

I had to find out what it meant.

There was only one person in the village who might possibly know—the Old Woman.

There was a crowd gathering outside the Old Woman's roundhouse—five or six villagers, and three of the monks from the monastery.

Aidan was there, so I tugged at the sleeve of his tunic. 'What's going on, Aidan?'

'Talorca!' he said. 'Oh, there's going to be trouble!' He was bubbling with excitement—or worry. It was hard to tell with Aidan.

'What do you mean?' I asked. 'What's happened?'

'Shh now.' He stood up straight. 'She's coming out.'

The Old Woman hobbled out of her roundhouse, leaning on a stick. 'Old Woman' was the title held by the leader of our half of the settlement, the people who didn't live in the monastery, and it doesn't have to mean that she's actually old, but in this case she was old—very old. Much older than anyone else in the village. Her hair was pure white, and it framed her wrinkled brow, rheumy eyes and near-toothless mouth. Her back was hunched, and she couldn't walk without her stick. Her voice was cracked and hoarse, but it had lost none of its sharpness or sting. She was a forbidding woman, a reminder of ancient days and the long darkness that waits for us all, and nearly everyone in the settlement was a little bit scared of her.

I wasn't.

The Old Woman was my favourite person in the whole settlement. She was the person I went to when I'd argued with my mother—which was often. She was the person I went to when I wanted to hear stories of the old days and advice about the future. She could be sharp with me, particularly when the argument with my mother had been my fault (which was more often than not) but she was never unfair. She held our community together, and always managed to soothe any tensions between the two halves of our settlement—the villagers and the monks. She had no official power over the monks, but you would often see figures in monks' robes paying her visits. Even the people who were terrified of her respected her enormously.

'Right!' she said. 'What's all this disturbance?'

Four people started talking at once.

She held up one crooked hand. 'Stop,' she said. 'You. Aidan. What's going on?'

'It's the Dalriadans,' said Aidan. 'They're coming.'

'What do you mean?' I interjected. The Old Woman frowned at me, and I looked down, muttering an apology. The Old Woman didn't like being interrupted.

'I saw them myself,' said Aidan, puffing out his chest. 'A group of them, on horses, coming up the coast from that new settlement.'

'It's a war band!' said one of the monks.

Aidan shook his head. 'I don't know if it's a war band or not,' he said. 'But they're definitely up to no good. Tell them, Talorca.'

I raised my eyebrows. Tell them about what?

'About the nets,' he prompted.

'Oh!' I said. 'Yes. Some boys in a coracle stole my nets yesterday. Aidan said it was probably the Dalriadans.'

'Who else could it have been?' said Aidan. 'It wasn't anyone from around here. I thought they were camping further down the coast, but it looks like they're heading for the village instead.'

The Old Woman sighed. 'I had hoped this was all behind us. If they are coming to attack or steal, there's not much we can do about it. We are too few, too old, too young, or too holy to fight them off. In times past, we had swordsmen and heroes, but now? Now we have nothing.' She straightened her back as much as she could, wincing with the motion, and a determined look lifted her jaw.

'I'll go and meet them on the road,' she said. 'Aidan, you and Talorca can come with me. There's no point meeting them with a mob if we can't fight them off.'

I swallowed my sudden knot of fear and nodded.

'I'll come too,' said one of the monks.

'You're not invited, Brother Cormac,' said the Old Woman.

'Someone should represent the monastery,' responded the young monk firmly. 'And if you've got the few, the old, and the young, you're going to want the holy to come along too.'

The Old Woman stared him in the eye for a long moment, and I wondered if she was going to take offence that he'd thrown her own words straight back at her, but when he met her gaze and didn't look away, she nodded.

'Come, then, holy man. Come if you want,' she said, then hobbled off to meet the invaders so abruptly that the rest of us had to scurry to catch up.

CHAPTER FOUR

Arrival

I COULD SEE THE DUST KICKED UP BY THE HORSES along the coast road, and before long the little band of invaders came into view. There were ten horses, eight with men in their saddles while the last two horses pulled a cart. At the sight of it, the Old Woman relaxed a little. A war band would have been more likely to bring a chariot than a cart.

We stood on the coast road, the four of us. An old woman, a girl, a boy, and a monk. As a garrison, we posed about as much threat as a litter of puppies. While we waited for them to approach, I looked back at our settlement.

The monks called it Port St. Colmag, while the rest of us called it 'The Port'. It was made up of two distinct parts—the monastery on the low hill above the cove, with its chapel and monks' cells and vellum-making and metalworking workshops surrounded by a ditch that did more to mark the extent of the monks' territory than to provide any sort of defence. Between the monastery and the beach was the

23

rest of the settlement—mostly farmers and fishermen, although since the storm three winters before that broke our two ships on the rocks, we did precious little fishing, and there were more women and children than men.

The Abbot was in charge of the monastery, while the Old Woman was in charge of the rest of the village. Of course, in reality the division wasn't quite that clear-cut. Several people from the village worked in the monastery making vellum and crafting metal items for the church, while some of the monks worked outside the monastery amongst the villagers, herding cattle and fishing. I didn't have a lot to do with the monastery—they were a little bit wary of women coming into their territory, which extended even to girls in their thirteenth summer—but I had been known to trade a little with them, particularly for shells that they crushed into lime for their vellum workshop.

In our whole settlement of perhaps a hundred people, there were maybe six or seven grown men who might be able to hold a sword or a club. Eight men on horses, with another two or three in a cart, would have been enough to put the entire village to the sword and burn the monastery to the ground. The Old Woman had told me of the wars of years gone by, when our people had fought with the Dalriadans. There hadn't been any trouble for a very long time, but our people had long memories.

The group of horsemen drew to a halt a short distance away. The leader seemed to speak to his men, then dismounted and walked towards us.

He was tall and broad, dark of hair and eye, his beard trimmed and tidy, with a short sword sheathed at his waist. It was only the sword that made him look at all warrior-like—for the most part, he looked like a nobleman or an extremely rich trader. His fur cloak was draped over finely-woven cloth that had been dyed a dark green, and a bright silver brooch glittered at his neck. As he drew closer I could see the brooch was intricately filigreed, with gold, silver and amber decorations. No-one in the Port owned anything as fancy as this brooch that he wore so casually.

I looked down at the brooch on my own cloak. It was a ring of bronze with a long pin, the head of which was delicately patterned with a knot-work design. When my father gave it to me I'd thought it the finest thing I'd ever seen, but now it seemed dull and primitive. This was a rich man. An important man.

He called out to us in a language I didn't understand.

'*Ciamar a tha sibhse?*'

The Old Woman responded haltingly.

'*Tha… sinn gu math, tapadh leat.*'

I hadn't realised she knew the language of the Dalriadans.

The lordly man replied, '*Feumaidh mi a bhruidhinn ris an maighstir na baile mu dheidhinn an stuthan cudromach.*'

The Old Woman opened her mouth, then closed it and sighed. 'It's no use. Language fades with the years, and I've lived so many without using it. Brother Cormac, can you translate?'

'Of course,' said the monk. 'He gives you greetings, and wishes to discuss some matters with the head man of the village.'

'Head *man*, indeed?' muttered the Old Woman. 'Tell him he can speak to me.'

Brother Cormac translated, and the Dalriadan nodded and responded.

'He says he is Nechtan mac Fergus, a Prince of Dalriada, and he wishes to settle here in Port St. Colmag.'

'Nechtan? That's not a Dalriadan name, is it?' said Aidan.

'No,' said the Old Woman, 'but Fergus is. His father must be Dalriadan, even if he himself bears a Pictish name.' She pondered a moment, as if trying to remember something. 'Ask him why he wants to settle here,' she said to the monk.

Brother Cormac translated. 'He says that he has heard that this is a place of good pasture and plentiful fishing, with room for men to make a home.'

'Ask him what he intends to do.'

Another unintelligible exchange took place, then Brother Cormac said, 'He says he would like to build homes in the village for himself and his kin, to raise cattle, to fish, and to grow crops.'

I looked over at the rest of the group. They were all men, apart from the three in the cart, who were boys—the same boys I'd seen stealing my nets! Their coracle was strapped over the load in the back of the cart.

I tugged at Aidan's sleeve again. 'Look,' I hissed. 'That's them. The boys in the cart—they're the ones who stole my nets.'

The tallest of the boys—the one with red hair—saw me pointing at him and nudged his friends. Then they all burst out laughing and shouting. *''S e cailleach uisge a th'ann, 'S e cailleach uisge a th'ann. Càit a bheil do phiorbhaig-feamad?'*

'What are they saying?' I asked. 'Tell me!'

'It's just nonsense,' said the monk.

'Tell me.'

'They're saying "It's the sea hag, it's the sea hag, where's your wig of seaweed?"' said the monk. 'That's all. Just nonsense.'

A sudden hot rage flushed my face. 'Get out!' I shouted, picking up a stone and throwing it at the cart. 'Go away!

Find some other village!'

Nechtan, startled by my attack, took a step towards me, his hand loosening the sword in his scabbard. Brother Cormac grabbed me as I stooped for another stone and pulled me back. He jabbered something at Nechtan, who frowned, but stopped drawing his sword.

'Stop,' said Brother Cormac to me. 'Please. You don't want to do this.'

All the fight drained out of me, all the anger faded, and I was left feeling hollow. Aidan spoke hurriedly with the Old Woman in a low voice, and she looked sharply up at the Dalriadans.

'Brother Cormac,' she said. 'Tell them they're not welcome here.'

'Are you sure?' asked the monk.

'Tell them.'

Brother Cormac took a deep breath and stepped forward, his hands clasped in front of him, respectful and submissive. I couldn't understand the words, but his tone was soft, his manner humble. Nechtan's hand didn't leave the sword-hilt, but eventually he shook his head and responded at length.

'Ah,' began the monk, turning back towards the Old Woman. 'He says you don't understand. He's not making a request. It is a royal command from your lord, Constantin mac Fergus, King of the Picts, who is Nechtan's brother.'

Nechtan stepped forwards and lifted his left wrist to show a broad silver bracelet marked with a crescent, a double-disc, and a snake with a broken spear—the clan symbols of our current King.

He wasn't just some rich foreigner. He was our King's brother.

Chapter Five

Council of War

'What's going to happen to us?' wailed Aidan. He was upset after the encounter—it had shaken him up more than the rest of us, even me.

We'd gathered in the Old Woman's roundhouse, Aidan and the Old Woman and Brother Cormac and me, after the Dalriadans had breezed past us on their horses. The image of the insolent expressions on the boys' faces as they went by on their cart was burnt into my memory. They'd ridden through the village to the north side, then started pitching their camp on the outskirts.

'We must tell the Abbot,' said Brother Cormac.

'What can the Abbot do?' I asked.

'I don't know,' said Brother Cormac, 'but he has to be told. I'll go now.'

'Bring him here, then,' said the Old Woman. 'I need to speak to him, and my old knees aren't up to the walk up the hill.'

The monk nodded, got up, and left.

I felt the need to fill the silence with a question. 'I don't understand,' I said. 'He's a Dalriadan. How can he be the brother of our King?'

'Oh, he's his brother all right,' said the Old Woman. 'He looks exactly like him.'

'But he doesn't even know our language!' I protested. 'I've seen our King. I've heard him speak. He came here five years ago, and talked with the men of the village.'

'King Constantin mac Fergus is the son of a Pictish princess and a Dalriadan father,' said the Old Woman. 'He has two brothers, Oengus and Nechtan. But when Fergus went home to deal with his estates in Dalriada, he left Constantin here in Pictland with his mother. He took Oengus and Nechtan with him, and they've been raised as Dalriadan princes, speaking their language and learning their ways. Constantin was raised to be our King, but the other two? They're foreigners by upbringing and custom, and half by birth.'

'But why has he come here?' I asked.

The Old Woman shrugged. 'Perhaps his brother wants him close in case of trouble. He and his men look like they know how to fight, and these are dangerous times.'

'Then why not invite him to court?'

'Do I look like I know the minds of kings and princes?' said the Old Woman. 'Perhaps he wants him close enough to help in times of trouble, but far enough away that he doesn't have to talk to him very often! It's not only the court that's in danger, anyway. Remember what happened to Hilltown?' The Northmen had attacked the village down the coast the previous summer—they'd been driven back to their ship, but the Hilltown people had lost most of their cattle, and two of their men had been killed. They'd faced real hardship trying to get through the winter with no meat, and not all of them had made it.

I shook my head. 'But what are we going to do?' I asked.

'We need to bring the people together,' said the Old Woman. 'We need to unite if we are to see off this threat. Brother Cormac is bringing Abbot Kilian. Aidan, stop wailing and make yourself useful. Go and fetch the heads of each household. Quickly now.'

'All right,' grumbled Aidan. He brushed the dust off his knees and headed outside.

When he'd gone, the Old Woman sighed. 'Ah, Talorca, my lass, what are we going to do? I'm too old for all this.'

'Can we not tell them that this is *our* home, and to find a place elsewhere?'

The Old Woman shook her head. 'You heard Nechtan.

32

They're here at the King's command.'

'But they're thieves! They stole my nets. They'll steal the very turf off your roof if you turn your back.'

The Old Woman said nothing, but sat as if deep in thought.

I made to say something more, but the Old Woman held up her hand. 'Quiet now, Talorca. I'm thinking.'

I scowled at her, then got up to look out the door. I'm not good at waiting around. I get fidgety and cross. I squinted into the bright daylight, but there was no sign of anyone arriving yet.

'Talorca. Come and sit by me.' The Old Woman tapped the bench beside her. 'Come and talk to me.'

'I thought you were thinking,' I said, unable to keep the sullenness out of my voice.

'I am,' she said gently. 'But sometimes my thoughts run more freely when my mouth and ears are engaged elsewhere.'

'What do you want to talk about?' I asked.

'Anything but the Dalriadans,' she said.

I remembered what I'd been coming to ask her, before the bad news had driven it from my mind.

'What do you know about the beast symbol on our clan stone?' I asked.

Surprise registered on her face—and if you knew the Old Woman, that was a rare event, and it almost made me smile.

'The beast? The horned animal?'

I nodded.

'No-one knows what it is,' she said. 'If it's meant to be anything at all, and not just a design, it could be a kelpie, I suppose.'

'What's a kelpie?'

'It's a river-horse. A monster of the seas and streams. At dusk it rises from the depths, takes the form of a horse, and lures you with the promise of a ride. When your hand touches its mane, it sticks fast and the beast races off to the water, where it drags you under to drown and be eaten. They say the only way to avoid being killed is to cut off your own hand.'

I shivered. 'That's horrible,' I said. 'It doesn't look much like a horse, though. Perhaps it's a beast.'

'A beast? I suppose you could say that. But does it matter? It's either one imaginary monster or another.' She pondered for a second or two. 'It makes sense that it might be a beast, though. You know the sword symbol on the clan stone?'

I nodded. Beneath the crescent was a two-bladed sword.

'My great-grandmother called that symbol the beast

34

sword. Although I'm not sure sword is the right word, either.' She pulled her stick towards her and made to get up. I stood and took her arm, helping her to her feet. 'You'll like this, Talorca, if you like old stories.' She shuffled to the back of her roundhouse, a mess of baskets and fleeces and broken tools from a lifetime of hoarding. She rummaged around in the clutter until she pulled out a heavy cloth. 'Ah! Here it is,' she said, and shuffled back to her bench. 'Unwrap that,' she said.

The cloth was old and stained, and smelled a bit strange, earthy and metallic. I unrolled it and out fell a sword about two feet long, split down the centre to make two parallel blades, with a leather-wrapped handle and iron crescent knob on the end. I lifted it up and stared at it with a slack-jawed expression that made the Old Woman smile. The sword looked like the symbol on our clan stone.

'My great-grandmother said this was a beast sword. But look,' said the Old Woman, 'the edge is blunt. It's never been sharp.'

'It's not much of a sword,' I said. The edge was as thick as my little finger. The sword couldn't have cut soft butter.

'The story goes that this sword summons a beast out of the wilderness. If you strike it on the right stone, it sings a clear, bright song that beasts find irresistible, and they are powerless to disobey you.'

'Really?' I asked.

'That's the story,' said the Old Woman. 'Go on! Try it!'

'But what about beasts?' I asked.

She laughed. 'I've accidentally banged it against stone a dozen times, my girl, and I don't see an army of beasts doing my bidding, do you? Between you and me, I don't think they actually exist.' She chuckled and gestured to me to strike the sword against the hearthstone.

I wasn't so sure that beasts didn't exist. Not after my encounter on the broch. But if the creature I'd seen *was* a beast, this would prove it, wouldn't it?

I took a breath and tapped the sword against the stone.

It made a dull clunk.

I tapped again, harder, but all that it produced was a louder clunk.

The Old Woman laughed. 'You should see your face,' she chuckled. 'You look so serious!' She wheezed with the laughter bubbling up inside her. 'Ah, my girl, you always cheer me up,' she said, drawing me into an embrace. 'And now my thoughts have been left alone to get on with their thinking, I know what we should do.'

I looked up at her old face, at her nearly-toothless grin and bright, shining eyes.

36

'If they're thieves, the best way to encourage them to leave is to steal *their* property. And you, my lass, you are going to be my thief.'

Chapter Six
The Hunt

'Where are you going?' shouted my mother as I ran out the door.

'Out,' I shouted back. As I raced down the cattle track to the point, I could hear her shouting something about fish or shellfish, but I wasn't interested. I had more important things to do, and I had no intention of telling her what I was up to.

The council of war hadn't gone very well. The Old Woman had been against the Dalriadans settling in the Port, but Abbot Kilian had insisted that it was the King's command, and it was the King as a "good and Christian man" who provided funds and resources for the monastery. The other heads of the households hadn't known which way to turn, but then my mother had spoken up and said that it would be good to have some more men about the Port, and that if they were good neighbours they'd be a benefit to us all.

My mother doesn't understand *anything*.

I'd tried to tell them about the Dalriadan boys stealing my net and fish, but I'd been shushed and told to keep quiet and let the grown-ups speak.

I ran to the crest of the small hill, burning off the last of the anger that had resurfaced when I thought back to the council. I could see the broch to the north, but in the weeks since the Dalriadans had arrived I'd seen no more of the beast. I presumed that it had wandered off back into myth and legend—assuming that I hadn't imagined it, anyway. The marks on my wrist had faded, and with them had vanished any evidence that the beast had ever existed.

I knew that the Dalriadans were planning a hunt, and that they'd be setting off not long after daybreak. I had no chance of keeping up with them on their horses, but they had a habit of leaving supplies in their cart while they chased after boar, returning once they'd made their kill. They'd then skin and butcher the animal before taking it back to the Port.

This time, they'd come back to find their skinning knives missing. Or their water-skins punctured. Or dung mixed into their midday meal. I hadn't quite decided what I was going to do.

I was key to the Old Woman's plan, and glad to do it.

If we made their lives unpleasant, if at every turn they found little irritations, perhaps in time they'd tire of the gritty taste of sand in their flour, or finding their stores of dried fish fed to their own dogs, and decide that some other village would make a better home.

The Old Woman had always said that I had a talent for mischief, so it was only fair that I put it to good use.

I dropped to my belly and looked down at the Dalriadans preparing for their hunt. Nechtan and his three sons were there, of course, along with two of the other men. Nechtan and the red-haired tall son had bows while the others had long spears. Spears are far better than bows when hunting boar from horseback, but it didn't surprise me that Nechtan and his thief of a son had chosen the wrong weapons for the job. My low opinion of them hadn't improved any over the weeks since they'd arrived.

Nechtan called out in his barbaric tongue, and they mounted their horses, leaving the cart hitched to a boulder. I pondered releasing the horse from its harness and setting it free to wander the point, but the stupid beast would probably stay where it was and chew on the tough grass. Besides, I didn't want to cause any injury to the animal by chasing it off; it wasn't its fault its masters were thieves and invaders. As I watched, the horse lifted its tail and deposited a heavy lump of dung onto the grass.

It was an omen. Dung in their food. That was the way to go. As the horsemen cantered out of sight, I slithered over the crest of the hill and, keeping low, ran towards the cart. I'd almost reached it when a shout rang out—a single word in the Dalriadan tongue, '*Mac-tìre!*', followed by a translation from one of the other men: 'Wolf!'

Wolf? There hadn't been a wolf on the peninsula for years. Not since the bad winter three years back that drove them down from the mountains in the west. I reached for my belt, where I kept the long knife my father had given me. It was better than nothing, but against a wolf? I didn't fancy my chances.

I needed to get to safety. The broch! The broch wasn't far, and was to the north, while the shout of 'Wolf!' had come from the east.

I ran to the broch, the fear of fangs and memories of howls in the long dark winter giving my legs strength. I scrambled up inside the walls, climbing as high and as quickly as I could, until I could peek above the top of the wall.

The Dalriadans on their horses were circling about. The horses seemed on the edge of panic, but for all their faults, the Dalriadans were good horsemen, and were managing to keep them under some kind of control.

A shout went up from one of Nechtan's sons, and they all turned to look. Low amongst the gorse bushes was a dark shadow in a predator's crouch. One of the men threw his spear, but it landed wide of the mark.

Nechtan dropped his reins, took up his bow and, holding tight to his jittery horse with just his knees, drew back the bowstring. An arrow flew straight and true, and hit the shadow with a noise I could hear even up on the broch.

A scream, a howl, burst out from the shadow, more like a fox than a wolf, and for the first time I wondered if the Dalriadans had been mistaken when they'd thought they'd seen a wolf. That wouldn't have surprised me—they were such braggarts and show-offs that they'd much prefer to tell a story of hunting a big dangerous wolf than a common fox. That would be why they'd shouted 'wolf' in our language—not as a warning to anyone nearby, but so that anyone close would know that they'd been chasing a deadly beast.

The scream from the animal cut off, and another arrow flew into the gorse.

A dark streak erupted from cover and raced across the ground: faster than any fox I'd ever seen; much bigger than a wolf; faster than a horse at full gallop. Two more spears flew after it, then a flurry of arrows as Nechtan and his son sent shaft after shaft into the undergrowth. I lost sight of the shape, then the Dalriadans must have, too, because the arrows stopped. Nechtan leapt from his mount and crouched over where the creature had been, touching the ground and looking at his fingers. Blood. There had to be blood.

Nechtan called out to his sons and his men, and they started looking around for the trail. I'd seen the animal head further out towards the point, but the Dalriadans had obviously lost sight of the animal in the thick gorse bushes, and started to move away, further inland. In ten minutes they'd disappeared from view.

I had no way of knowing how long they'd take in their hunt, so I'd missed my opportunity to cause mischief with their cart. I'd have to go home and try another day.

I clambered carefully down the broch, making sure of my footing. I was paying so much attention to each step that I almost didn't notice the panting shape at the bottom of the broch.

It was the monster—the beast—curled up on the rubble in the centre of the broch's floor, an arrow deep in its shoulder. Thick, almost black, blood darkened his grey coat.

One eye opened and stared at me, and an almost inaudible whimper came from its throat.

Chapter Seven
Healer

I stood in shock for a moment.

The beast snarled, and I took a step back. He turned his long snout to snap at the arrow in his shoulder. He couldn't reach it.

He needed my help.

I slowly reached out and put a hand on the beast's shoulder. I looked at the wound. The arrow had driven deep into the muscle, and when I touched the shaft I could feel it vibrate slightly as the arrowhead ground against the bone within. The beast growled in pain.

'If I pull it out, it's going to start bleeding,' I told him, as if he could understand me. It was *already* bleeding, but it would get much, much worse without the arrow sealing the wound.

What could I do? I needed to get help from the village. But some of those were the people who'd attacked him. The ones who'd thought this strange-looking creature was a wolf. Hardly the sort of people you could trust to help.

I starting pondering who I *could* ask to help. Aidan was a shellfish gatherer who wandered up and down the coast collecting mussels and limpets for his family. He'd taught me all about the tides, and knew which coves gathered the most flotsam and jetsam, but livestock? He knew next to nothing about livestock. My mother knew about looking after animals, but she and I hadn't been speaking much since the Dalriadans had come to the Port. The Old Woman knew everything, but there was no way she'd be able to walk the miles to the broch.

What about Brother Cormac? He was in charge of the cattle for the monastery. He had to know something about healing wounded animals.

I tore a strip of cloth off the hem of my dress and packed it around the arrow shaft where it entered the wound. 'That should stop the flow of blood,' I said. 'Try not to move. I'll be back as soon as I can.'

The beast closed its eyes and seemed to lose consciousness. I ran out of the broch and started to sprint back along the cattle track to the Port. It was a good couple of miles, but I'd run the distance a hundred times before and I knew how to pace myself.

As I jogged along, I rehearsed what I was going to say.

'Come quick, there's a monster with an arrow wound?'
Somehow I didn't think that would do the trick. By the time
I'd made it to the entrance to the monastery, I still hadn't
decided what to say.

'Hello!' I called out to the first monk I saw, my breathing
still ragged from my run. 'Have you seen Brother Cormac?'

He scowled at me, then pointed to the vellum workshop.
I ran up to the entrance and paused. The stink coming from
inside was horrible—calf skins were being soaked in lime,
then scraped and stretched and dried to be turned into
pages for books. The scraped-off slivers of flesh managed to
find their way into every tiny crack on the stone floor and
lie there rotting, no matter how hard the vellum-makers
tried to keep their workshop clean.

I took a deep breath and stuck my head inside.

'Brother Cormac?' I called.

'Yes?' came the response.

'I, uh,' I began. I still hadn't come up with the words.

'Out with it, girl,' said the monk. From my mother, or the
Abbot, those words would have had more of a barb. Brother
Cormac seemed more amused than anything else.

'There's a... an animal, and it's injured. Can you come?'

'Can't your mother help?'

'I can't find her,' I lied. 'And it's urgent. He's... it's bleeding.'

46

The monk straightened up from his scraping. 'Can you carry on here?' he asked his assistant, who nodded. 'Then I'll get my things,' he said to me. 'Wait for me at the boundary. You're not really supposed to be in here, you know.'

I nodded, and rushed back to the other side of the ditch.

While I waited, I paced up and down. Would the beast still be alive when we got back? Would it be there at all? Would it think that I'd gone to fetch the hunters who'd attacked it?

'Which way?' asked Brother Cormac, waking me from my worries.

'Out by the broch on the point,' I said.

The monk raised an eyebrow. 'That's quite a distance,' he said.

'Please,' I said. 'The animal is badly hurt.'

'Then we'd better get moving,' said the monk.

'Just up here, is it?' asked the monk as we drew close to the broch.

I nodded. I hadn't trusted myself to say anything on the journey to the point. I still didn't know how the monk was going to react when he saw the beast: the imaginary creature from the stone.

47

I gestured to the broch, and the monk made his way over the crumbled fallen stones to the doorway. 'He's inside,' I said at last.

It was bright outside, and dark within, so it took our eyes a moment or two to get used to the gloom. I felt a warm rush of relief come over me when I saw that the beast was still there, and his sides were moving like a horse panting after a gallop. He was still alive.

'Talorca,' said Brother Cormac uncertainly, 'what is this?'

I shrugged.

'I was expecting a calf,' said the monk.

'Please help him,' I said. 'He's been hit by an arrow. The Dalriadans thought he was a wolf.'

The beast's eyes were closed. He seemed to have passed out. Perhaps it was just as well.

'It looks dangerous,' said Brother Cormac, looking at the beast's teeth, clearly visible as his jaws were parted to let his tongue loll and pant like a dog.

'He's not,' I said, not entirely convincingly. 'I'll hold his head if you look at his wound.' I sat by the beast and pulled his head into my lap. He groaned as the arrow moved against its bone. 'I think the arrowhead is stuck in the bone,' I said.

'I sincerely hope not,' said the monk, pulling his tongs and knives and pots of herbs out of his bag and laying them down next to the beast. He touched the arrow shaft and tried to rotate it. The beast stirred and snarled, lips pulling back from its dangerous-looking teeth. The monk froze. 'You're going to have to hold its mouth shut,' he said.

'He won't bite you,' I said.

'Talorca, if you had an arrow wound this deep, and I did to you what I'm about to do to this animal, *you'd* bite me.' He pulled a length of cloth from his bag and passed it to me. 'Wrap it around its snout. Keep it tight. And keep hold of its head.'

I did as I was told, then looked in horror as he pulled out a long, narrow blade. 'What are you going to do?'

'I can't turn the arrow shaft,' he responded. 'Which means one of two things. Either the arrowhead is embedded in the bone, in which case there might not be much I can do, or it's merely that the arrowhead is too broad to turn. I'm going to cut down alongside the shaft, widening the wound, and see if I can free the arrowhead.' He looked at me. 'There's going to be a lot of blood.'

'I've seen blood. I've seen animals slaughtered.' I lifted my chin defiantly.

The monk nodded, then pushed his blade down into the wound.

For all my brave words, I had to look away, and then my

words were forgotten entirely as I hung on to the beast's head with all my strength. Brother Cormac leaned his weight on the beast's body to hold it still, and between us we managed to hold him steady enough for the monk to slice down the shaft of the arrow.

A horrible wailing noise escaped the beast's bound jaws, and his eyelids flickered.

'Nearly there,' said the monk, sweat dripping down his brow even in the coolness of the broch shade.

I held the beast's head tighter.

'Good news,' said Brother Cormac. 'The arrowhead is rubbing against the bone. It's not actually stuck.' He dropped his long-bladed knife onto the stone and reached for a pair of narrow tongs. 'I should be able to pull the arrow out now without causing any more damage.' He pushed the tongs into the wound then paused. 'Just a moment.'

'What is it?' I asked.

'This isn't good.'

'What?' I demanded.

'I've seen this before. If the arrow hits the bone, sometimes it causes the muscles to spasm with such force that the tip of the arrowhead gets bent like a fish-hook. If I just pull it out, it could tear at the animal's flesh. If it hits an artery or rips a tendon, it could be very nasty.'

'What can we do?' I asked.

'Here,' said the monk. 'Can you reach over with your right hand? Give me your finger.'

'What? Why?' I asked, reaching out my hand.

He took my finger and plunged it deep into the wound. 'Feel that?' he said. 'That's the bent tip of the arrow. Keep your finger on that to cover it while I pull the shaft out.'

I felt the sharp point on my finger-tip and shivered.

'Whatever you do, don't let go,' said Brother Cormac. Slowly he tightened his grip on his tongs and pulled steadily. My blood-slicked finger threatened to slip from the jagged point so I pushed hard, letting the point sink into the pad of my finger.

After what seemed an age, the tip of the arrow came clear of the bloody flesh, and I let out the breath I'd been holding. The beast's head was still at last, but I could feel the breath hissing in and out of his lungs; he'd passed out.

'Good,' said Brother Cormac, dropping the arrow to the ground. 'Now, hold the edges of the wound together while I stitch them up.' He pulled out a curved needle and threaded a bit of twine through its eye. Blood welled from the wound as I pushed the jagged edges together, and the monk dribbled a bit of water from a small jug over the injury so he could see what he was doing. The needle slipped through the flesh, and he tugged the twine tight.

At length, he sat back. 'I've done what I can,' he said, then asked the question he'd obviously been desperate to ask since he first clapped eyes on the beast. 'What *is* it, Talorca?'

'It's a beast,' I said, softly.

He laughed and got to his feet. 'What do you mean? A beast? Like a monster? It doesn't look like any monster I've ever seen.'

'You've seen a monster?' I asked.

'Well, I've seen them in books,' he said. 'When monks get tired of illustrating manuscripts, they draw all sorts of things in the margins.' He looked at the beast. 'But they don't look like that.'

He poured a bit of water over his hands to clear off the worst of the blood and shook them.

'Will he be all right, now?' I asked.

He shrugged. 'I don't know. It was a deep wound. Do you intend to look after the animal?'

I nodded.

'Then keep the wound clean. Keep the beast fed. That's the best chance you can give it. And keep it away from hunters.' With that, he turned and left.

'Thank you!' I called after him.

The beast whimpered in agreement too tiredly and softly for the monk to hear.

CHAPTER EIGHT
Sabotage

'HELLO?' I CALLED OUT INTO THE DARKNESS. 'I've brought fish.' I waved the turbot, hoping the beast would catch its scent.

Limping with one leg, the beast hobbled out of the dark into the evening light.

He was walking! I'd been bringing him fish and washing his wound for two weeks, and he'd never managed to get onto his feet before now.

I looked around to make sure there was no-one in sight. The last thing I wanted was for the Dalriadans to see him and chase him down with their spears and arrows. He was in no condition to run, and I didn't think I'd be able to defend him with my little knife.

'Come on, then,' I said, and laid my hand gently on his injured shoulder.

The cliffs on the southern edge of the peninsula weren't very big—perhaps twenty feet or so. They were so steep they actually had an overhang at some points, and no-one I knew had ever risked climbing them, not even to collect the seabird eggs from the nests that speckled the cliff's surface. But the cliffs did provide a pleasant spot to sit and eat and watch the waters of the firth. I breathed in the sweet honey smell of the yellow gorse flowers, through which I could detect the salt tang of the sea spray below.

I unwrapped some oatcakes and a sliver of dried beef for my own meal, and placed the freshly-caught flat turbot on the grass in front of the beast. He snapped at the fish, tossed it into the air, and swallowed it down whole. I nibbled more slowly on my own meal.

'Look,' I said, pointing out over the water. 'Dolphins.'

A school of the creatures burst through the calm sun-dappled surface of the firth, their dark shapes silhouetted against the bright sea.

'You look a bit like a dolphin, you know,' I said, looking sidelong at the beast. It was the nose, I think. Long and sharp and inquisitive. 'Do you swim? Do you miss the sea?' He certainly seemed to have a taste for fish.

With barely a wince, the beast lifted the paw of his injured leg and uncurled the long claws, then spread them wide. A pale webbing, like the skin on a seabird's feet, stretched between the toes.

It certainly looked like he was made for swimming. He watched in silence as the dolphins disappeared into the distance, his grey eyes almost exactly the colour of the sea, and I wondered if one day he'd just swim away and I'd never see him again.

I looked over my shoulder. 'The sun's going down,' I said. 'Mother will be wondering where I've got to. And why my net isn't producing much turbot these days.' I sighed. 'Let's head back.'

I'd barely stood up when the beast growled and pointed his snout out to sea. I dropped to my belly beside him.

It was the blasted Dalriadan boys in their coracle again. They wouldn't find my nets this time; after they'd stolen them, when I'd finished making my new nets I hadn't been so stupid as to lay them in the same place. I'd put my nets further around the northern side of the point, in a deep channel that wasn't quite as fruitful as my original spot. Better to take home three fish than to catch five and have them all stolen, along with their net.

'They're heading for my old fishing spot,' I said. 'The nerve of them! They're going to lay my own nets in my own fishing spot!' Anger gripped my chest like an angry fist. Their arrogance infuriated me.

They weren't going to get away with it.

The sun had passed below the horizon, and the short night had begun. The sky still showed a hint of purple light in the west, but the stars were coming out bright and crisp in the east. It was going to be a clear night, but the moon was barely a sliver and would set in a couple of hours. I hoped I'd be able to do what I needed quickly, as I'd have a difficult time avoiding ditches and rabbit-holes if I had to walk back by starlight alone.

'Talorca,' came a familiar voice.

'Brother Cormac,' I responded, nodding politely. I'd actually been avoiding him since he helped with the beast, which made me feel ungrateful. I'm not sure why I'd been avoiding him. Perhaps I wanted to keep the beast as a secret for myself.

'How's your animal?' he asked.

'A lot better,' I said. Then, after a pause that was *slightly* too long, I added 'Thanks to you, of course.'

'I'm glad,' he said. He looked like he wanted to say something more, but I wanted to get away and meet up with the beast.

'Good evening, then,' I said, and turned to leave.

'Talorca,' he said. 'I may have some books you might want to look at.'

'Books?' I said. 'I can't read.' What a silly thing for him to say. Only monks can read.

'I know,' he said. 'But there are some very illuminating pictures. They might cast some light on your animal.'

I looked at him.

'If you're interested, come and see me tomorrow morning.'

'Where?' I asked, against my better judgement.

'The chapel,' he said. 'Our library is in the crypt.'

I nodded. 'Tomorrow, then,' I said.

'Tomorrow,' he agreed. He looked thoughtful.

I rushed off towards the point before the light faded. I didn't want the monk to be poking his nose into the beast's business. I was grateful for his help with the arrow, but I was afraid that my thoughtless mention of the word 'beast' had set him down a path that would lead to trouble for me and the beast. I should have told him that the beast was a rare breed of goat!

About half a mile from the point, on the south-east coast, there was a track that led down to the rocky beach and the base of the cliffs that extended the rest of the way to the point. The beast was waiting for me on the shoreline, as if he knew what I intended to do.

I took off my cloak and outer layer of clothing. My father always taught me to dress in layers, the better to keep out the cold wind that blew across the point and could freeze your limbs, even in summer. I had a long woollen dress on over a thin tunic and breeches, so I pulled the thick dress off over my head. The sea was going to be cold—even at midday in summer, it could bring a chill to your insides—but the heavy dress would weigh me down. I placed my boots on my pile of clothes so they wouldn't blow away, then stepped gingerly onto the jagged rocks with my bare feet.

I put a toe into the cold water and shivered.

The beast looked out to sea, then back to me.

'Yes,' I said. 'I'm going to swim out to their nets.'

He came to stand near me, and bowed his head.

'What?' I asked. He looked up at me, then bowed his head again. 'You want me to climb on?'

For a second I felt an irrational shiver. This was how kelpies got their prey. You climbed on their backs, got stuck to their manes, then were dragged under the sea to drown. Drown and be eaten.

'How do I know you're not a kelpie?' I asked. That was silly. Of course he wasn't a kelpie. Kelpies didn't exist.

But then, beasts didn't exist either.

I took a tentative step forward. Then another. When I took a third, I realised that my feet had already made the decision, and walked right up to the beast. He bowed his head, lifting those long curved horns into the air, and I clambered onto his back. He lifted his head, and the horns came to rest against the tops of my thighs, holding me tightly in place.

I was stuck. As surely as if I'd touched a kelpie's magical mane.

I took a deep breath to try to calm myself down. I could feel my heart racing in my chest.

The beast loped towards the water, his limp giving him a strange rocking motion. His claws clicked over the rocks, then splashed through the rock-pools, then finally he plunged into the cold dark sea up to his shoulders and began to paddle like a dog, his snout lifted out of the water. On land he was still limping, but in the sea he seemed perfectly comfortable, as if his wound didn't bother him at all. The strokes of his powerful limbs lengthened, and before long we were further out to sea than I'd ever swum on my own.

I guided him with my knees and soon we were swimming up the coast. I clenched my jaws to stop my teeth from chattering, and soon a pale cow bladder, almost luminous in the starlight, appeared ahead of us. This was where the boys had set their stolen nets, more or less in the same area I used to place them, a little bit further out to sea so you couldn't reach them from the coast, even at low tide.

I reached out and grabbed the bladder. I tried to pull up the net, but the Dalriadans had weighted it with heavy stones.

'Let me think a minute,' I said.

If I couldn't steal the net back, at least I could make sure they couldn't have it. I pulled out my knife, cut the float away, and threw it as far as I could. The dark lines of the net disappeared below the surface. They'd never find it now.

'Let's go back,' I said, then stopped dead. There was a shadow on the surface of the water, barely fifty yards from me—the sawtooth blade of a shark's fin, slicing slowly through the waves and heading right for us. 'Quick!' I said. 'Come on!' I nudged the beast with my knees, but he was fixated on the shark like a hunting dog that had seen a squirrel.

'We have to get back to shore!'

The beast growled and paddled *towards* the fin, which was still gliding through the water, slicing back and forth as the shark sniffed out its prey. I'd seen the damage sharks could do—Domnall Pegleg from Hilltown could tell you all about that. I was keen to keep all of my limbs attached, so I pulled hard on the beast's horns and tried to steer him towards shore. 'Come on!' I begged, but the beast shook his head free of my grip and paddled faster, a growl rumbling through his entire body, getting louder and deeper until I could feel it in my guts more than I could hear it through my ears.

And still we headed for the shark.

'Please!' I pressed my head against the beast's, but he wasn't going to change course. The shark was a challenge, and he wasn't going to back down.

The shark was barely a dozen yards off now, so close I could just about make out the huge shadow beneath the surface of the water. I imagined the mouth opening to reveal rows upon rows of knife-sharp teeth...

And then, with a swish of the huge tail, the shark turned around and headed back the way it had come.

The beast stopped in the water, stared after the retreating shark for a long minute, then allowed me to guide him back to dry land.

Just how dangerous *was* the beast, if even huge sharks were afraid of him?

Before long we were back on shore, and even though I'd been shaken up by the encounter with the shark, I grinned.

We'd done it. We'd started fighting back against the boys.

'Thank you,' I said to the beast. He growled softly in reply.

I looked up at the crescent moon, which was sinking fast towards the horizon. 'I'd better get home,' I said. 'But tomorrow evening, we'll keep an eye out and see what happens when those rats come back and try to find their net.' I grinned again. 'They're going to be disappointed!'

CHAPTER NINE
The Book of Beasts

I'd never been in the chapel before. It was a small rectangular building, with a stone altar and a cross at the far narrow end. The doorway was low, and even I had to duck to avoid bumping my head.

'This way,' said Brother Cormac.

'Where?' I asked. He was pointing at a blank wooden wall.

'Look,' he said, smiling, and pushed at the wall. The wall swung smoothly open, revealing a flight of stone stairs leading down. He picked up a candle from a wooden box and lit it from a thick slow-burning candle on a tall iron candlestick.

'Should I take a candle, too?' I asked. One little candle wasn't going to provide very much light down in the crypt.

'No!' said the monk. 'No,' he repeated, more calmly. 'There are a lot of precious books down here. I don't want to risk any more flames than are necessary.'

'Why keep them down there in the dark, then?' I asked.

'For safety,' said the monk. 'Follow me.'

The crypt was nearly as big as the chapel above, nearly thirty feet long, with stone walls and a closely-paved floor. Wooden shelves lined each wall, and crammed into those shelves were shining gold and silver cups and crosses, glittering in the candlelight. And books—shelf upon shelf of books, some new, some old, all filled with secrets.

'What are all these things?' I asked.

'We prepare the necessary supplies for new monasteries,' he said.

'Like grain and meat and water?' I asked.

'No,' smiled the monk. 'You can get those anywhere. No, these are the most important elements of a new monastery. A book of the gospels, a cross, a chalice, and a paten.' He gestured to the shelves, with their mysterious glittering treasures. I presumed the cups and plates were the chalices and patens he was talking about. I don't know why he didn't just call them cups and plates.

'Are these the books you wanted to show me?' I asked.

'No,' he said, and gestured to the back wall of the crypt. In the dim candlelight I could see another shelf of books, no different to my eyes from the shelf of gospels. He put the candle down on a table, and pulled out a thick and dusty volume. 'This is the history of our monastery, going back to its founding by St. Colmag nearly a hundred and fifty years ago. In those days, saints walked the earth, spreading the gospel and performing miracles. You've heard of St. Columba, of course?'

I shook my head.

'I've got a life of Columba here somewhere...' Brother Cormac looked around. 'But that's beside the point. Before the monks came, your people were pagans, worshipping strange gods and wild animals, and following wizard-priests. The first Christian saints to walk these lands had to defeat the wizards on their own terms, so they performed miracles to prove that our God was the true God, and so drive out the wizards and the demonic beasts. There's a story they tell about St. Columba, who came across a group of people burying a man by the shores of Loch Ness. The man had been grabbed by a water beast and dragged under the waters of the river. St. Columba asked one of his followers to swim across the river, but when the water beast appeared and made for the man, the saint called out to the monster and made the sign of the cross. He cried out "Go no further. Do not touch the man. Go back at once." The beast came to a sudden halt, like it had been pulled back with ropes, and swam away in terror. The local pagans were amazed, and converted to Christianity at this sign of the power of Christ's servants.'

'Why are you telling me this?'

'Because there's a similar story in the histories of this monastery about St. Colmag.'

'Which is?' I prompted, although I was already pretty sure that I had an idea about what he was going to say. I *knew* I should never have mentioned the word 'beast'.

'Here,' said Brother Cormac, opening the book at one of the earliest entries. In the flickering candlelight the dark lettering seemed to dance, and the colours of the illuminations around the border were reduced to various shades of orange. 'In the first year of the monastery, a beast appeared on the point, horrible in appearance, and terrorised the monks as they tried to gather stone to build this chapel. The cattle stampeded, and two of the monks were slashed by the beast's sword-like claws, cutting their flesh to the bone. St. Colmag was convinced the beast was a devil sent to test the faith of the monks, and set out to confront it, armed only with a cross and a copy of the gospels.'

'What happened?' I asked.

'It doesn't say,' said the monk. 'All it says is that after the chapel and crypt were completed, the attacks stopped, and the beast was seen no more.'

'That's not quite as impressive as your story about Columba and his monster,' I pointed out.

'No, I suppose not,' said Brother Cormac. 'But then, St. Columba was the greatest of all the saints who have ever walked these lands, and no-one has ever been his equal. But the important thing is here, a few pages later. When they started building the cells and workshops a year later, St. Colmag issued a decree that the monks were to obtain the stone only from the quarry down the coast.'

'I don't understand,' I said.

'What I think happened is that the monks were taking stone from the broch and using it to build the crypt. Look here,' he said, lifting the candle. 'At this end, along the floor, are big grey drystone blocks. Just like the ones from the broch. All the rest of the crypt, and the chapel itself, is made from quarried and shaped red sandstone.'

'I still don't understand,' I said.

'I think the builders tried to take stone from the broch where your wounded animal was. And it tried to defend its nest. When St. Colmag realised what was going on, that the beast was defending its territory, he stopped the monks taking stone from the broch, and ordered them to use quarried stone instead. Because the monks weren't threatening its nest any more, the beast stopped attacking.' He looked me right in the eye. 'Look at this drawing in the margin. It's a beast like the one on the clan stone, but more than that—it looks just like the wounded animal in the broch. Look—where the clan stone has whorls at the end of the legs, the book shows curved claws. I'm worried that the beast that harassed the cattle and attacked the monks is the same sort of beast that you've been looking after. And that means that it's a dangerous, dangerous animal.'

'He's not dangerous,' I said.

'It's not a "he",' said Brother Cormac. 'It's an animal. A wild animal. And I think it could hurt you badly if you threatened it.'

'Any animal is dangerous if you threaten it,' I said. 'Would you startle a cow when its horns were pointing right at you? Would you stand behind a horse and slap its rump?'

'Of course not,' said the monk. 'But I've had experience with cattle. I know how to behave around cows. I know how not to spook them, and how to avoid being gored or kicked. What I'm saying is, we don't know *what* might make your animal attack. The monks who founded this monastery had no idea that the simple act of taking stones from a ruin would cause it to attack them.' He put his hands on my shoulders. 'Please. Be careful. I don't want to see you get hurt.'

'You don't understand,' I said. How could I tell him that he was wrong about the beast? That it could understand me in a way that no other animal could? I didn't want Brother Cormac to run and tell the Abbot that there was a devil-beast living out at the point.

'Perhaps I should speak to your mother,' he said.

'No!' I said.

'Well, promise me you'll stay away from the beast.'

I looked him in the eye. If I didn't promise, he'd tell my mother, and the Abbot, and who knew what would happen then?

'I promise,' I lied.

CHAPTER TEN
Coracle

As I trudged down the hill from the monastery, my thoughts filled with beasts, I saw Nechtan swaggering along the road ahead of me, his fancy cloak flipped back over his shoulder and one hand resting casually on the hilt of his sword. There was no reason for him to be holding onto his sword—my father had always told me that swords were tools like any other, not ornaments or toys. Nechtan wore his sword like a badge of self-importance.

He was talking loudly in his uncouth tongue, bending the ear of a slender dark-haired woman walking at his side, and occasionally calling out to the youngest of his sons who trailed along behind, carrying a basket. I felt sorry for the poor woman. Nechtan's voice sounded loud enough from where I was standing. She had to be deafened by the oaf.

I stopped in my tracks when the woman laughed gently, turned to Nechtan, and put her hand on his arm in a gesture that could only be of fondness.

The woman was my mother.

I felt sick. What was she doing? Going on a walk with the enemy? I was trying to make up my mind whether to follow her when, to my relief, she turned towards our home and Nechtan and his son carried on towards the beach.

Still, something about the way she'd been fawning over the fool made me uneasy. It had been three years since my father died. Three years since he and his boat had crashed onto the rocks at the point. My father had been twice the man Nechtan was. He'd never had fine clothes or golden brooches or a fancy sword; the only thing of value he'd ever owned had been his boat, and that had been his undoing, in the end. But still. He'd been a man of modesty and integrity, not a braggart and a show-off.

My mother wasn't exactly old, but she *was* a widow, and a respected woman in our community, so how was it that she was acting like a girl, giggling at this oaf and fondling his arm?

I glanced at the sun. It was nearly time for the boys to bring in their nets, so I pushed the unpleasant thoughts from my mind and headed for the point.

The cliffs overlooked the spot where the boys had laid their nets. My nets. The evening sun was dipping towards the horizon and painting the world crimson.

I felt rather than heard the beast creep up beside me, and I turned to look at him.

Brother Cormac's book had made me think about the beast. What if *he* was the creature from the founding days of the monastery? I had no way of knowing how long such creatures lived, so maybe he'd been hiding on this peninsula for hundreds of years. He didn't seem threatening to me, but perhaps I was fooling myself. Perhaps if Aidan hadn't startled him on the broch, he'd have attacked me. If I hadn't been feeding him since he was wounded with the arrow, maybe he'd have seen *me* as a meal.

But then, he was nearly completely healed now, and still he didn't attack me. If I could call anyone a friend, it was the beast.

Maybe that said more about me than it did about the beast. Wild Talorca, whose only friend was a monstrous beast from legends! My mother sometimes called me a little barbarian. Perhaps she was right.

The beast pointed out to sea with his snout.

The coracle with the three boys was skimming swiftly across the sea towards the nets. The tall red-haired boy

72

was propelling the tiny boat with strong strokes with his oar, first one side, then the other. The two smaller boys sat behind him and chattered to each other in annoying, high-pitched voices that carried over the sea even to my ears. I couldn't understand a word, of course.

The red-haired boy snapped something at them, and they fell silent. He placed the oar carefully in the bottom of the coracle, then looked around. I'll say this for him—he was in pretty much the exact spot where he'd laid the net. His seamanship wasn't bad at all.

Such a pity that there was no net to be seen!

Coarse voices raised in anger drifted across the water to me. One of the smaller boys was pointing closer to shore, while the other was pointing further up the coast towards the point. The tall boy was shouting and pointing down at the sea next to the boat. 'It was right here!' I imagined he was saying.

The argument got angrier and angrier.

The red-haired boy, after getting his breath back, was standing up in the coracle. The other two were shouting at him, probably asking him to sit back down—by now the coracle was rocking alarmingly. He was shaking his fist. One of the smaller boys tried to pull at the tall boy's shirt, then, with no warning, the coracle tipped up and dumped

73

all three of them into the sea.

I burst out laughing. The boys floundered in the water, splashing as they tried to right the coracle and kept getting in each other's way. They clambered back into the little boat, nearly capsizing it again, then started shouting at each other when they realised the oar was missing.

They spotted the oar, then paddled to it using their hands. By this point I was creased double with laughter, and my cheeks ached from the grin on my face. I must have been laughing quite loudly, because the red-haired boy looked up suddenly, scanning the cliffs until he saw me standing there. The beast was crouched down, well hidden, but I was silhouetted against the setting sun. I waved cheerily and they responded with a torrent of incomprehensible gibberish.

Satisfied, I gave them one last wave, then left the cliffs to go to the other side of the point and bring in my own nets from their sheltered cove. I gave the beast two flatfish, then put the rest of my catch into my bag to take back to my mother.

As I walked back to the village, I decided that I was going to have to learn some of the Dalriadans' language. It would be so much more satisfying to understand what they were saying when they ranted at me.

I could speak to Brother Cormac about that. He knew several languages—my own, the Dalriadan tongue, and Latin, that I knew of. Perhaps he'd be willing to teach me. Although perhaps a monk wasn't the best person to teach the sort of language the boys had been using.

Chapter Eleven
A Dinner Party

I WAS ALMOST SKIPPING AS I MADE MY WAY HOME. For the first time in months, I felt in control. I'd won my first real battle with the Dalriadans, and, while I knew it would be a long, drawn-out war, I could finally see some hope that I'd win in the end. This was just the beginning. I had so many plans. So many ideas.

I hummed a tune to myself as I pulled aside the curtain on our doorway and ducked inside.

'Mother! I'm home!' I called.

'Talorca,' responded my mother. 'Come in. Sit down. We have a guest for dinner.'

Sitting next to the hearth, his cloak folded up and used as a cushion on my father's chair, was Nechtan.

'What's *he* doing here?' I said.

'Talorca,' said my mother, the warning clear in her voice. 'Sit down. Dinner will be ready soon.'

She stirred the pot on the fire, and the glorious scent of

beef and herbs wafted towards me. My nose twitched. Beef! We had precious little of our dried beef left, and it would be months until we slaughtered the next of our small fold of cattle.

'I said sit,' said my mother. I'd been standing, staring at the interloper, frozen in fury.

I sat, as grumpily as I knew how.

My mother said something to Nechtan, '*Chan eil innte ach trioblaid,*' and he laughed.

'You speak their language?' I said, surprised.

My mother shrugged. 'A little.'

'But how?' I asked.

'Never mind. Help me dish out.'

I glowered at her and poured a little of the beef into a bowl and handed it towards Nechtan.

'A bit more than that, Talorca,' said my mother. 'Show some generosity to our guest.'

I glared at her.

'Talorca,' warned my mother, so I poured a little more into the bowl and gave it to Nechtan. He grunted something in his vulgar tongue and grinned at me.

My mother handed him a spoon. He lifted the bowl to his mouth and scooped a great mouthful directly into his face.

'Mmm,' he grunted, his mouth still full of beef.

He ate like a pig. 'I don't think much of his princely manners,' I said.

'Don't be rude,' said my mother. 'That's how they eat at court.'

'How would *you* know?' I said.

Nechtan said, '*Tha i ag ithe mar 's gur e rabaid a th' innte,*' and my mother laughed. It sounded fake and forced.

'What did he say?' I asked.

'Never mind,' said my mother. 'Now, eat your beef and help me keep our guest company.'

I ate the small portion in my bowl, which was all I was given after the pig Nechtan had scoffed most of it. I made sure to eat as delicately as I could, in the hope I could make him ashamed of his manners.

He didn't notice, of course. He stuffed his face, talked to my mother with his mouth full, and laughed like a coarse buffoon.

My mother laughed along with him, and I felt my anger growing. It's true, I'd barely heard her laugh since my father died, but her laughter sounded *wrong*. Unnatural, even. It was like she wasn't just talking in another language, she was *laughing* in a different language, and I couldn't understand it at all.

Eventually, Nechtan got up, bowed in a mocking fashion to me and then more sincerely to my mother, and took his leave.

When he'd gone, my mother sank back onto her seat and seemed to deflate. She sighed and glared at me. 'I don't know what you're playing at, Talorca, but if we hadn't had a guest I'd have given you a proper talking to.'

'He's not a guest,' I said. 'He's an interloper. An invader. A bully and an oaf.'

'He was a *guest* in our *home*, and deserved your respect.'

'Respect? What respect does he show us? He doesn't even speak a single word of our language!'

'Languages are harder to learn when you're older,' said my mother. 'Or so I've heard.'

'How difficult would it be to learn the words for hello or goodbye or thank you?'

My mother frowned at me, then shook her head sadly. 'You might have a point,' she said. 'But people like Nechtan aren't used to making adjustments for other people.'

'I don't understand why he was here in our home.'

'No,' said my mother, 'you probably don't.'

'Well?' I said.

'I chose to invite him. I thought it was important to get to know our new neighbours.'

'They're not *neighbours*,' I began, but my mother held up a hand to silence me.

'No, no, they're not neighbours, they're invaders and interlopers and devils and I don't know what else.' She shook her head. 'I know you don't like them, but they're here to stay.'

'Not if I have anything to do with it,' I muttered.

'What do you mean by that?'

'Nothing,' I said, and stormed out into the night.

I stood outside my home, wishing that what I felt was anger. It wasn't, though. A heavy lump had settled in my chest and I almost felt like I wanted to sob to break it up. I felt like I wanted to run, or curl up and sleep, or both at the same time.

I hated the Dalriadans. I hated them with all my heart. But the anger that had kept me going, the fire that had sustained me, had been replaced by black, smothering misery.

I didn't know why. What did it matter that my mother had invited Nechtan for a meal? I'd still won the battle of the fishing nets. I still had plans for more mischief. It shouldn't have affected me so much.

But it had. He'd been in *my* home, eating *my* food, laughing with *my* mother, sitting on *my* father's seat.

My *father's* seat. How dared he? If my father had still been alive, he would never have allowed it.

I felt the dampness of rain on my cheeks, and wiped it away, but when I looked up I could see the pinpricks of stars spread across the endless black of a cloudless sky.

CHAPTER TWELVE

Language Lessons

'I MUST SAY, I'M PLEASED that you want to learn the language,' said Brother Cormac.

'We should be able to understand what our neighbours are saying,' I said.

'Oh, I totally agree,' said the monk.

'How did *you* learn their language?' I asked.

'It's my native tongue, Talorca.'

I was taken aback. Brother Cormac was one of us. A member of the village, even if he did live in the monastery. He was as much part of the village as my mother and Aidan and the Old Woman. 'But you've always lived here,' I said.

'I've lived here a long time,' said the monk. 'But not always. I arrived here not long after you were born, when I was still a boy. I came from the great monastery at Iona, where I received my training, and before that from the misty Winged Isle, where I was born. Both are within the kingdom of Dalriada.'

'Oh,' I said.

'You'll find that most of the monks are from the west,' said Brother Cormac. 'Many of us look to Iona as our mother church.'

'But you all speak our language,' I said.

'We should be able to understand what our neighbours are saying,' said the monk with a smile. 'Amongst ourselves, we speak Latin, the language of the church. With our neighbours, we speak your language. Until the Dalriadans came, I'd actually nearly forgotten my own native tongue, it had been so long since I spoke it.' He smiled at me again. 'Which is one of the reasons I'm glad you asked me to teach you,' he said. 'It will be nice to use the language again. It reminds me of my childhood home.'

Brother Cormac was an excellent teacher. He was patient and understanding when my tongue struggled with the strange sounds of the Dalriadan language. There were some sounds that he made that I couldn't even tell the difference between for a long time. Eventually my ears got used to the sounds, though it took longer to train my mouth to form them correctly. When I struggled to copy the sounds the monk made, I asked him to describe how he was making the sounds. If Brother Cormac could form the sound with tongue, teeth, palate, and lips, then I could, too. The monk was intrigued by this concept, and came up with a system of symbols to represent the various sounds. When I struggled to pronounce a word, he'd scratch the signs onto a piece of slate, and it would help me sound out the word.

'You know, this is a form of reading,' he said one day.

'No it isn't,' I said. Reading and writing were for monks. Normal people couldn't do such things.

'It is,' he said. 'Look, here's the symbol I use for the "tih" sound, where your tongue is tapping behind your front teeth. In the Latin alphabet it would look like this: "T". Then the symbol for the "ah" sound would be "A".' He continued to scratch letters on the slate, matching them to the symbols we'd been using for the lessons. 'We can string the symbols together. What does that say?'

I looked at him as if he were daft. 'I can't read,' I said.

'Look. Try.'

'Ta... lor... talorca.'

'Excellent!' he said. 'You can now read your own name.'

'It's that simple?' I said. I'd thought for years that reading and writing were a great mystery, that they were secrets that only monks knew. And now it turned out that it was a simple matter of matching symbols to sounds. I shook my head in amazement.

'Let's continue,' said the monk.

84

I nodded, and we went on with the lesson. My slowly-growing ability to understand the Dalriadan language was starting to give me an idea for more mischief, and I was keen to get started.

I hadn't been able to work out where the boys hid their coracle. It was typical of thieves that they were worried about someone stealing *their* property. With the help of the beast, I'd managed to cause some more trouble as the summer days shortened and autumn approached; but what I really wanted was to smash or steal their little boat. The Old Woman kept suggesting schemes that would make the Dalriadan men feel unwelcome, but I had a grudge against the boys, who still kept calling me the 'sea hag', so I concentrated on annoying them as much as possible. They'd obtained another net from somewhere—probably stolen—but I had decided that I wouldn't play the same trick twice. No, it was the coracle that was my main target.

All I knew about the coracle was that the boys took it down the coast after they'd done their fishing. There were too many people milling about for me to follow—the shore usually had Aidan and some monks combing the beach for shellfish, so it was too much of a risk. The beast came with me on all of my expeditions, too, and I didn't want to bring him any closer to the settlements. I'd told Brother Cormac that the beast had disappeared one day, so that the monk wouldn't feel obliged to tell my mother.

The beast was my secret friend. My only friend.

I continued my lessons in the Dalriadan language with the monk, in the hope that it would help with eavesdropping on the boys. Although to tell the truth, I enjoyed the lessons. Brother Cormac was a good teacher, and he had an enormous store of tales from history and myth that I found fascinating. Not just about our own people, or the Dalriadans, but about the Northmen, too, with their wolves and ravens and strange gods. The monk knew a few words of the Northmen's tongue that he'd learned from a nephew of one of the Earls who'd been a hostage at the Dalriadan court.

'A hostage?' I asked.

'A hostage is somewhere between an honoured guest and a prisoner of war,' explained Brother Cormac. 'Erik's father, the Earl, had traded the boy to the Dalriadan king in exchange for a group of prisoners from a war band who'd been captured in a raid. The warriors went home, and Erik remained at the Dalriadan court as a token of friendship.'

'His own father handed him over to his enemies? How could he?'

'One boy isn't worth very much compared to a band of warriors,' replied the monk. 'And Erik was treated like a prince. He sat at the King's table, went hunting with the King's sons, and was given a monk as a tutor along with the other young princes.' Brother Cormac smiled. 'I considered him my friend,' he said.

'But what would have happened if the Northmen had raided again?'

The monk frowned. 'I don't know. The King was fond of Erik, but I don't know whether that would have stopped him from punishing him according to the laws.' He shook his head. 'I don't know what happened to him, in the end. He might have gone home, or he might still be there.'

'Or, he might...' I began.

'No,' said Brother Cormac. 'Let's not start thinking of that.' He changed the subject, and I could never get him to talk about it again.

His friendship with Erik meant that Brother Cormac could recite some lines of the Northmen's poetry—it sounded bleak and stormy like the northern seas, and when he translated it for me it turned out to be mostly bloody and violent stuff about ravens feeding on the bodies of the slain.

I remember some of it to this day, and it can still make me shiver.

How are you, ravens?
Where are you coming from,
With your beaks bloody
As morning breaks?
From your talons hangs torn flesh,
The stink of carrion is on your breath.

I'd also learned to read and write a few words of Latin, although the monk had warned me not to tell anyone; Latin was only for monks and nobles, and certainly not for people like me.

My mother seemed pleased that I was learning the language of our interlopers. She'd been their main supporter with the rest of our community, and had some misguided idea that their arrival had been good for us. I couldn't get the image of my mother fawning over Nechtan out of my head. I didn't believe she was thinking clearly. The Old Woman had stopped speaking to my mother. They'd never been the best of friends, but for them to be so openly hostile to each other was new and strange.

I don't think my mother knew how completely I'd taken the Old Woman's side. If you're going to keep a secret from your mother, it helps if you don't speak to her very much. Mothers have a way of sniffing out lies. Better to say nothing at all.

CHAPTER THIRTEEN

The Coracle Thief

I MADE IT A POINT TO WALK PAST THE DALRIADAN camp each day, hoping to use my new knowledge of their language to pick up useful information. I kept my head down and avoided the jeers of the boys, who took every opportunity to point and laugh and call me 'sea hag'.

One early autumn day, when the sunlight was turning amber and the eastern breeze was turning chill, I was taking my usual route past their camp. I stopped in my tracks.

When the Dalriadans had first arrived, they'd stayed in cow-hide tents over wooden frames. Big tents—substantial tents—but tents nonetheless. As the year had worn on, they'd built two roundhouses similar to the one I shared with my mother. But they'd obviously decided that those weren't enough.

The men were using stakes to mark out the perimeter of a huge building, twice the size of my home. Bigger even than the Old Woman's house. That wasn't right. The Old

Woman was our leader, our matriarch. She had the largest roundhouse because she was the Old Woman. It was a matter of prestige. It was a matter of *respect*.

'Do you like it?' came a voice from behind me.

I turned and looked at the red-headed boy. I scowled at him. I hadn't realised he knew our language.

'It's going to be our great hall,' he continued.

I frowned at him.

'A great hall,' he said, 'is where a leader and his warriors sleep and feast and entertain each other with tales of heroism.'

'I don't see any leaders or warriors,' I said. 'Just thieves and vagabonds.'

'Aha!' he laughed. 'She *can* speak!'

'I can speak,' I said. 'I choose not to speak to the likes of you. How do you know our language, anyway?'

'Oh, I know many tongues,' said the boy. 'I spent a lot of time at my grandmother's court. I speak your language, and my own, and Latin, and the language of the Britons of Strathclyde.' He looked at me, his grey eyes narrowed. 'My name is Finn. Like the hero.'

'What hero?' I said.

'Surely you know of Finn mac Coull?' he said. 'The greatest hero of these islands. He tasted the salmon of knowledge, defeated the fairy folk, and led a band of warriors and hunters the like of which the world had never seen before, and will never see again.'

'Sounds like a lot of nonsense to me,' I said.

'What would you know?' he said. 'My father and his men are the modern-day descendants of my namesake and his band, and some day *our* stories will become legend, too.'

'You place a lot of importance on something as trivial as a name,' I said.

'My name,' sneered Finn, 'has *history*. It gives me something to live up to. What's *your* name, anyway? Or shall I just call you Sea Hag?'

'Talorca.' I glared at him. 'Not that it's any of your business.'

He frowned at me. 'Talorca? You're Mael's daughter?'

I nodded. 'Mael is my mother, yes,' I said. I hadn't realised he even knew who my mother was.

He looked around. 'I can't spend all day talking to you,' he said. 'You'd better go. I have things to do.'

He turned and made for his brothers. I had no idea why my name, or my mother's name, had stopped him in his boasting. He called out to his brothers in his own language.

'Thalla dhan a gharadh agus faigh an curach.'

Go to the cave and get the coracle. The cave! They hid

92

their coracle in a cave! That made sense. There were two or three caves in the hollow cliffs further down the beach. I didn't go there very often—they were filled with rock-pools that were refreshed only at the highest tides, so usually the stagnant pools were yellow-tinged and smelly and didn't hold even the smallest anemone or hermit crab. They'd be ideal to hide a coracle if you wanted to keep it close to the sea, but out of sight.

Now that I knew about their hiding place, their coracle was safe no longer.

The tide was high, and lapped against the entrance to the cave. The water came up to my waist, and I clenched my jaws against the cold so my teeth wouldn't chatter. The beast paddled like a dog alongside me.

He looked into the cave, then looked back at me. He looked reluctant to go any further.

I nodded, unwilling to open my mouth in case it betrayed how cold I was.

The beast pulled himself out of the water into the cave and sniffed.

'It smells bad,' I agreed. I pulled myself up beside him. 'It could be the stagnant rock-pools. Or it could just be the boys.'

The beast snorted as if he understood my joke. His eyes were huge in the gloom, their normally slitted pupils expanding to circles. He padded across the rocky floor of the cave. The coracle was sitting upside-down on a shelf of rock, out of the damp stinking pools.

It was bigger than I thought. I'd never actually seen it up close—out on the water, with the three boys squeezed into it, it had seemed tiny, especially compared to the clinker-built boat that had belonged to my father. But now, looking at it, I wondered how I was going to steal it on my own.

I pulled at the coracle and it moved a little. 'Perhaps if I can drag it out to the sea, it'll float away,' I mused out loud. No. It might end up a short distance down the coast.

I took out my knife. 'I'll have to slash it,' I said. The coracle's hull, made of hide, would be easy enough to hack through with a sharp enough blade, and the knife my father gave me was extremely sharp. I'd honed its edge a few days before.

It took a lot longer than I thought, but I slashed each panel with long, jagged tears. There was no way they'd repair it without re-skinning the whole boat. By the end of it my arms were aching and I had a huge blister on the palm of my hand. My neck hurt from constantly looking around at the opening to the cave, worried in case the boys came and found me. But then, what could they do to me if I had a fierce beast by my side? I was invincible!

The last of the sun dipped down below the horizon, leaving only a red-orange afterglow in the sky to show where it had been. I liked watching the sunset from the top of the broch, but today, it had been especially beautiful.

The boys wouldn't have a clue what had happened to their coracle. I'd have to tell the Old Woman about what we'd done. Even if she'd rather I'd spent my time making the men unwelcome, I was sure she'd be pleased with what I'd done to the boys.

'Thank you,' I said to the beast, who was lounging on the wall. 'I couldn't have done it without you.' I'd never have dared go into the coracle's cave without my friend at my side.

He didn't know it, but I suppose it was in the beast's own interests to drive the Dalriadans away. As long as they stayed, there was a chance they'd hunt him down— and maybe next time he wouldn't be so lucky. Perhaps on some level the beast understood this. Maybe he realised that the enemy of his enemy was his friend.

Sometimes I was tired of the fighting, but I knew it

could only end when the Dalriadans were driven out. I knew the Dalriadans had fought my people many times in wars going back hundreds of years. If people couldn't get along with each other, what chance did we have to get along with the beast?

'I wish people could live together in peace,' I said, then laughed. That was a strange statement for a girl who had been doing her best to disrupt the peace with her neighbours for the past few months!

But of course, I didn't mean *them*. I meant people in general, not the Dalriadans in particular.

No, I certainly didn't mean the Dalriadans. They'd invaded my village, hurt my friend, stolen my nets, and set themselves up as lords over the rest of us. With the slashing of the boys' coracle, I'd struck the first real blow against them. I had no doubt that I was on course to drive them out of my home.

Chapter Fourteen
More Arrivals

THE NEXT MORNING, AFTER I'D CHECKED ON THE CATTLE for my mother, I went to see the Old Woman.

'Hello?' I called as I entered her house, and peered into the darkness.

'Over here,' came a quiet voice.

The Old Woman was lying on her bed, a blanket up to her neck. I'd never caught her sleeping before. She was always the first to wake and the last to go to sleep, and she'd often told me that sleep was a waste of time at her age.

I frowned. There was no fire in the hearth, either.

'Shall we have some light?' I asked, and knelt to build a small fire from a bundle of sticks. I pulled my flint and steel from my bag and within a minute had coaxed a few sparks to catch hold on the dry tinder and spread to the sticks. When they'd built to a nice fire, I'd go out to the peat stack for a couple of blocks that would burn slow and warm.

I looked up at the Old Woman. She'd closed her eyes,

97

and looked to be in pain, her jaw twitching as she gritted her teeth.

I knelt by her and waited.

At length, she opened her eyes.

'Can I get you anything? Should I fetch anyone?' I asked, hoping she wouldn't hear the worry in my voice.

She shook her head. 'Help me up, lass,' she croaked.

'Maybe you should lie down,' I suggested.

'Help me up,' she said, sounding more like her normal self. She leaned onto one elbow, so I had no choice to pull her up into a sitting position. The blanket fell from her. I picked it up and placed it around her shoulders. It wasn't cold, but the Old Woman leaned towards the fire as if starved for warmth. The flickering light illuminated her face, and I'd never seen her look so tired.

'What's wrong?' I asked.

'I'm old,' she said, as if that explained everything. 'I'm tired.'

I opened my mouth to ask again, but I realised that I didn't want to know the answer. Or rather, I already knew the answer. She was ill. And at her age, any illness could mean that the end was close. Tears pricked at my eyes, and I looked away into the shadows so she wouldn't see.

'So, then,' she said quietly, 'how has your mischief making been going?'

I shrugged, unwilling to trust my voice.

'I suppose it doesn't really matter,' said the Old Woman. 'I fear that we've lost.'

'Don't say that,' I said. 'I'm not giving up.'

She shook her head slowly. 'You haven't heard, then.'

'Heard what?'

'Nechtan came to see me yesterday. Another twenty of his kinsmen are coming to stay.'

'They can't!' I said.

'There's nothing we can do,' she said. 'Ah, Talorca my lass, I fear that I've been a bad influence. We should know when to bow to the inevitable.'

I shook my head, scattering a few teardrops that welled from my eyes, despite how tightly I was holding them shut.

'We've done all we can,' she said. 'Maybe it was the foolish idea of an old woman set in her ways. At my age, you'd think I'd be able to let go of the past. But somehow I've never been able to forgive the Dalriadans for what they did all those years ago.'

'What did they do?' I asked.

'It's better forgotten. And once I've gone, there will be no-one left to remember it. There will be no-one to bear a grudge. It's better that way.' She sighed. 'Your mother will make a better Old Woman. She'll bring everyone together. That's what we need now.'

'My mother's a fool,' I said. 'She's been taken in by these... these *men* with their fancy brooches and big houses. She's not like you. She just doesn't understand.'

'Your mother is no fool,' she said. 'And she's not one to be taken in by precious jewellery. She's probably never told you, but she spent her childhood at court before coming to the Port. She grew up as a kinswoman of the King, with fine clothes and all the fancy brooches she could ever want, but left that all behind when she married a fisherman. If she'd married someone of high status like a foreign prince, her children might have been in line to be king. You've never wondered why you were called Talorca? You were named after your mother's cousin, King Talorc. You're of royal blood, more or less.' She tugged at my tangled hair. 'Although I daresay *most* princesses comb their hair once in a while.'

I'd never known that and I didn't know what to say. I realised that I'd never given much thought to my mother being an actual person with a history and a life rather than... well, my mother. I'd certainly never thought of myself as being a kind of princess.

'Go away, now, Talorca. I'm tired.' She lay back down on her bed and stared at the fire.

'I'll put a peat on the hearth,' I said.

'No,' she said. 'Leave it. I want to watch the fire fade and go out.'

I didn't know what to say to that, so I left.

I lay on the sand, staring at the sky. I had a little fire burning on the beach, and I was cooking some limpets and winkles in its embers so I didn't have to return home for the evening meal. I couldn't face my mother.

I picked a hot limpet out of the ashes and flicked the meat out of the shell with the point of my knife. Carefully I sliced off the black gut sac and chewed the salty lump of meat.

The beast padded up the beach, a turbot in his snout.

'You caught one!' I said. It looked like he was fully healed, now he could hunt for himself. The thought made me a little sad, and I wondered if he'd need my help for much longer. He tossed the fish into the air and swallowed it whole with a snap of his jaws.

I burned my fingers on a winkle from the fire and used a stick to pull the flesh out. I dropped the shell into the pile with the others. The monks used the shells to make lime for their vellum workshop, so there was no point throwing the empty shells away.

The beast stretched out on the sand next to the fire.

'I think it's over,' I said to the beast. 'There are more Dalriadans coming. About twenty of them. We've failed.'

Twenty. Twenty more big, smelly, uncouth, obnoxious Dalriadans. Where were they all going to live? In the great hall, I supposed.

But that gave me an idea. The Dalriadans had put the roof on the hall only the other day, but what would happen if the new group turned up, and there was no roof on the hall? They'd probably have to turn around and go home.

And turf roofs do burn terribly easily, don't they?

CHAPTER FIFTEEN
Fire

THE PROBLEM WAS GOING TO BE FINDING A TIME WHEN the hall was empty and unguarded. It took me two whole days of observing the comings and goings of the Dalriadans to come up with a plan. Unfortunately, I was going to have to set the fire on my own—it was far too close to too many people for the beast to help me.

I tried to explain to the beast what I was going to do, and that he couldn't help. I couldn't tell how much he'd understood, but he'd had a strange look. There was a lot going on behind those eyes.

I sat in the shadow of the clan stone, my back to the stone beast that was the image of my partner in crime and waited for my opportunity. Most of the Dalriadans tended to take a walk along the beach after their evening meal each night, before their drinking and singing got under way. That would be my opportunity.

A wolf howl broke the evening air, then another. The

panicked calls of cattle answered it. A clatter came from the great hall as the men rushed to see what was going on. The wolf howled again, closer this time. A shouting and scuffling followed, then the clang of steel weapons as the Dalriadan men headed off in search of the wolf. The big brave men of the great hall of heroes couldn't resist a hunt like that!

It had to be the beast. The more I got to know him, the more I became convinced that he could understand just about anything I said to him. I hadn't been sure that I'd made myself clear, but it sounded like not only had he understood, but the beast had decided to help, and even managed to elaborate on the plan, and imitate the howl of a wolf to draw them off.

It was a pity for the men that there wasn't a wolf. The beast would lead them far away. I hoped he was going to stay safe. But he had the advantage of knowing exactly where the men were coming from, so I was sure he'd manage to stay one step ahead.

When the noise of the men faded, I got to my feet and headed for their hall.

The hall was right on the edge of the village, and the

Dalriadans had dug a shallow ditch around the perimeter to set it even further apart. Our village was now split into three parts—the monastery, the village itself, and the Dalriadan encampment. I didn't understand how the Old Woman thought my mother was going to bring these different cultures together. Oh, I suppose the monks weren't a problem. We'd lived alongside them for generations without any real friction, but the Dalriadans? They'd been here barely weeks and had disrupted *everything*.

I had to get rid of them.

I jumped the ditch at the rear of the hall and knelt on the muddy ground. I dumped the contents of my bag onto the ground, and started to put together my fireball.

First, a heavy ball of dry woven long grass. I tied a long piece of wet twine around its middle and pulled it tight, leaving a long tail. Then I poured a little lamp oil from a jar over the ball of grass—that would help it burn.

I struck spark after spark from my flint until the ball lit, then picked up the end of the wet twine. I hoped the string would hold for at least a few seconds.

I swung the fiery ball around my head, faster and faster. The flame drew a bright circle in the air, and I got ready to let go and send the fireball sailing onto the roof...

When without warning I was knocked to the ground,

and the fireball sailed harmlessly into the ditch.

'What are you doing?' shouted Finn.

I struggled to my feet and spat at him.

'Are you mad?' he said, his face a mixture of anger and confusion. 'You could have burnt the hall down!'

'That was the idea,' I said, and swung a punch at his head. He swayed backwards, caught my wrist in his left hand, and pulled it up behind my back, twisting me around. I struggled for a second until I felt the cold iron of his knife against my throat.

All the fight drained out of me. I was barely aware of Finn shouting for help. I didn't notice when the rest of the Dalriadans turned up, or when my mother and the other villagers appeared. I think there was a lot of shouting, a lot of accusations on both sides, but it all seemed so far away and muffled, and I couldn't make out what was being said over the sea-roaring in my ears. I have a vague recollection of Aidan trying to pull me away from Finn and the Dalriadans, of swords being drawn and more shouting and pointing, of Nechtan fishing my soggy fireball out of the ditch and holding it up for all to see. I don't know how long it all went on for.

But the next thing I remember clearly is my mother walking up to me, tears making clean rivulets in the dust on her cheeks, trying to say something, finding no words, and turning away in deafening silence.

CHAPTER SIXTEEN
Prisoner

DO YOU EVER RECALL SOMETHING YOU HAVE DONE, even a long, long, time ago, and your heart clenches in the shame of what you did?

The first time in my life I had that feeling of utter remorse was when I woke the next morning on the dirty floor of an old cow-byre and, after a few blissful seconds of utter blankness, the memory of the previous day flooded in. I curled into a ball and tried to shut the world out. Tried to forget everything. Tried to wish yesterday out of existence.

It didn't help. No matter how tightly I closed my eyes, in my head I could see the fiery circle of the torch spinning around.

The rickety door of the byre was pulled open and I could see a Dalriadan on guard outside, his back to the door, one hand on his sword-hilt. Nechtan, Finn, and my mother were standing there, faces grim. My mother's eyes were red from crying, but the set of her lips told me that they'd been angry tears.

Nechtan gestured to me to get up.

'What's happening?' I croaked. My mouth and throat were dry. I couldn't remember the last time I'd had even a sip of water. I could still taste burning grass in my mouth.

'There's to be a trial,' said my mother.

'But...'

She shook her said. 'I think you should stay quiet,' she said. 'You've caused enough trouble. Nechtan wanted to send you off to face the King's justice.'

A lump of fear settled in my stomach. I knew it had happened in the past, but I'd never seen anyone from our village being sent away to face the King in a trial. It hadn't happened within my lifetime, anyway. The King's justice was reserved for the worst of crimes, and I suddenly realised that what I'd done could have serious consequences. Possibly fatal consequences.

'Your mother managed to convince him that it wouldn't be necessary to trouble the King,' said Finn. 'But my father insists on justice. We will have a trial, here in the village, in the hall you tried to destroy.'

'Get up, Talorca,' said my mother.

'Now? The trial's happening now?'

She nodded.

'Don't think about running,' said Finn, putting a hand on the knife in his belt. I felt a chill line across my throat as I remembered him holding the blade against me. I shook my head to indicate that I had no intention of trying to escape.

They led me from the cow byre to the Dalriadan hall, where most of the villagers were already waiting. I could see Aidan, and Brother Cormac, and Abbot Kilian.

'Where's the Old Woman?' I asked.

'She's ill,' said my mother.

'But she's the Old Woman,' I said. 'She's the leader of this village. She should be in charge of the trial.' My only hope was that the Old Woman would take my side, and soften any punishment that Nechtan tried to give me.

My mother shook her head. 'She can't,' she said. 'Besides, your crime was against the Dalriadans, so Nechtan will act as judge.'

'Nechtan?' I said. 'But he doesn't even speak our language! What right does he have to judge me?'

My mother stopped in her tracks and turned to face me, her nose almost touching mine. 'You tried to burn his hall,' she said. 'I'd say he has every right to judge you.' She backed off a little and sighed, the anger falling from her. 'Oh, Talorca. You've brought shame on me. On our family.

On this village. You've brought shame on all of our people.'
She stared me right in the eye. 'You've brought shame on
the memory of your father.'

That last barb stabbed me right in the heart.

Chapter Seventeen
The Trial

Finn stood up in front of his father's high chair. 'Nechtan mac Fergus, Prince of the Picts, Lord of the Dalriadans, brother of Constantin King of the Picts, will judge this trial in accordance with the laws of God and Man.' He looked at me. 'As the accused does not speak our tongue, I will interpret for my father.'

A shred of pride returned to my heart. I didn't want this boy, this upstart, this *thief*, speaking for me. I stood and said, carefully, in the Dalriadan tongue, '*Chan eil feum aig duine sam bith a bhith a' bruidhinn a' chànain agam.*' I do not need someone to speak my language.

Nechtan looked at me in surprise, and almost smiled. 'That is well,' he said. 'We will be able to proceed more quickly.'

I have to admit, I was beginning to regret my boast. It was only later, when I'd learned more of their language, that I knew for sure that he'd said 'proceed more quickly' and not 'put you to death' or something like that. But once I'd said it, I couldn't take it back.

The trial did proceed very quickly after that. Finn gave his evidence of how he'd caught me red-handed, they held up the part-burnt torch, still dripping ditch mud, for everyone to see, and then the other Dalriadans started telling stories of other crimes they suspected me of carrying out. I was surprised to find that I'd only done about half of them, but of course I couldn't say that without admitting to the other half. I was being accused of every misplaced turnip, every stray calf, every snagged tunic and worn-out boot.

They'd decided to pin on me every last tiny misfortune they'd suffered since they'd arrived.

'Now you have heard the crimes of which you are accused, have you anything to say?' asked Nechtan.

I stood up.

What was the point? I hadn't done half of what they'd accused me, but I'd done enough. Worst of all, I *had* tried to burn down their hall. My fate was in the hands of my enemies, and I didn't even deserve their mercy, even if they were inclined to give it.

I cleared my throat. 'I...' I began. What could I say? Concentrating on the unfamiliar words and trying not to make any mistakes, I continued. 'I am sorry. The day you arrived, I wanted you to leave. I tried to drive you away. When I heard that more of you were coming, I thought, if I burn the roof of your hall, you will have nowhere to live, and you will leave. I... I understand that you want to punish me. And I accept.'

Nechtan nodded. 'That is well spoken,' he said. 'And I agree. You must be punished.' He sat back in his chair, looking like the lord and leader of men he was. 'You must be banished from this village.'

'No!' said my mother. 'She's just a girl! You can't banish her!'

'What would you have me do, Mael?' said Nechtan. 'She is dangerous. She bears no love for my people.'

'We are *all* your people,' said my mother. 'We all live here. We share these lands, these seas, and this village. If you have any intention of making a life here, you have to realise that.'

'It's all right, mother,' I said tiredly. I wondered where I would go. I wondered how far I'd have to go before Nechtan would feel safe.

'It is *not* all right,' said my mother. 'You are my daughter.' She turned to Nechtan. 'How would you feel if it was your son who was being banished?'

'My son has committed no crimes,' said Nechtan.

'That,' said the Old Woman, 'is where you are wrong.' She shuffled into the hall, her face as grey as the blanket around her shoulders. She paused and leaned against her staff. Aidan jumped to her side and took her arm, steering her to a bench. She sat stiffly and closed her eyes for a second. Then her eyes snapped open and she scanned the room. 'Cormac? Where are you?'

'Here,' said the monk, touching her on the shoulder.

'Stand by me. Help me with the language if I ask. I am tired, and my tongue may rebel at speaking Dalriadan words.'

'Of course,' said Brother Cormac.

'Have you asked the girl why she hated you from the first day?' she asked.

'She hates all of our people,' answered Nechtan, shrugging.

'But *why*?' responded the Old Woman. 'She hates you because the first time she saw any of your people, your son, Finn,' she pointed at the boy, 'was stealing her fish and her nets.'

'Nonsense,' said Nechtan immediately, then looked at his son. The expression on Finn's face must have surprised him. 'It *is* nonsense, Finn?'

Finn shuffled his feet and mumbled, 'It was only a few fish.'

'You see?' said the Old Woman. 'Then do you know why she carried out all those crimes?' Nechtan looked blankly at her. 'I will tell you. She stole and sabotaged and caused trouble because *I told her to*.'

The room erupted in a dozen voices clamouring to be heard.

Nechtan held up a hand and called for silence.

'You? You told her to do all those things? You told her to burn my hall?' The anger in his voice was almost a physical presence in the hall.

'Yes. No. I told her to do all the other things, but the plan to burn the hall was all her own. If she'd told me about it, I'd have stopped her, but really, can you blame her? She's only a girl. I set her on the path, so it's my fault if she followed it further than I intended.'

'But why?' asked Nechtan.

'Because I *hate you*,' spat the Old Woman. 'I hate you and your son and your kin and your whole nation. Your people stole my husband from me in the battle of Dunadd, and for that I will never forgive you.'

'The battle of Dunadd?' said Nechtan. 'But that was more than sixty years ago. And it was a battle *your* people started, and won.'

The Old Woman shook her head. 'My husband was

sent in to your fortress to offer terms, and your people stabbed him in the gut. *That's* why Oengus mac Fergus utterly destroyed Dunadd. Your people have no honour. No justice.'

'That's not true,' said Nechtan. 'Many things happen in war. But we are not at war.'

The Old Woman sighed and shook her head tiredly. 'Don't listen to me. This is why you can't blame the girl. I passed onto her my own anger and my own hatred. I've nursed my anger for too long. I can't let go of it. But perhaps she can.' She looked at me. 'Talorca, lass, I'm sorry. You don't deserve to be banished. If anyone deserves it, I do.'

'No!' I said. 'You didn't *force* me to do anything.'

'I know,' said the Old Woman. 'But I encouraged you.'

How could I tell her that none of it had been her fault? That if I'd listened to her advice, it was because she was telling me exactly what I wanted to hear? That I'd joined forces with a beast, a monster, a wild creature of legend and followed *his* example more readily than I'd followed hers? That the thought of these men coming into our village and taking the place of my lost father was like a knife in my heart?

The words stuck in my throat, and I couldn't find a way to bring them out. I knelt in front of her and took her bony hand in my own. She bowed her head, her eyes creasing in pain.

'Help me up, Talorca,' she said.

I took her arm and she stood up straight. Her upper arm was so thin my hand nearly wrapped all the way around it.

'Nechtan mac Fergus, you have heard my words,' she said, her voice clear and thin like mountain air. 'There is fault to be found with many, including your son, and none more so than with me. You will not banish the girl.'

'Who are you to say what I will or will not do?' said Nechtan.

'I am the Old Woman of this village, and if you intend to make a life here for you and your kin, you will respect that,' she said.

Nechtan glared at her, anger burning beneath his brows. She lifted her gaze to meet his without flinching.

'Very well,' he said at last. 'The girl will be punished. But not banished.'

The Old Woman nodded.

'As for you...' said Nechtan.

'You can't do anything to her,' I interrupted. 'She's old. She's not well.' I took a step forward. I didn't care what he did to me. I couldn't let him punish the Old Woman.

118

'*You* are in no position to bargain, fire-starter,' said Nechtan.

'But she's...' I heard the Old Woman give a little groan, heard her staff slip from her grip to clatter against the stone slabs. I spun around and tried to catch her, to break her fall, but she hit the ground before I could reach her. Her eyes rolled back in her head so only the whites were showing through narrowed eyelids, and a strange slackness took hold of her features.

Chapter Eighteen
The Last Story

THE NEXT FEW DAYS WERE HARD. The Old Woman remained in her house, hovering between consciousness and oblivion, neither fully awake nor managing to rest. No-one could do anything for her. Abbot Kilian prayed at her bedside for hours at a time, while my mother and Brother Cormac took turns mopping her brow and trying to dribble a few drops of water past her lips.

I still had the threat of my punishment hanging over me. The Old Woman's speech followed by her collapse had thrown the whole trial into confusion, and no-one had told me what my punishment was going to be. I'd been allowed to return home, although that was a mixed blessing, as my mother hadn't spoken a word to me since the trial, and the silences between us had been almost physically painful.

I'd tried to get away to find the beast, the only real friend I had left, but Finn and his brothers had been shadowing my steps ever since the trial, and I couldn't risk them finding him.

I spent most of each day at home, in near-darkness, pushing twigs into the embers of the hearth-fire and watching them blacken and burn.

'Talorca?'

I looked up at the sound of Brother Cormac's voice. He stood at the doorway, holding the cow-hide curtain aside. I got to my feet. 'How is she? Is she...?' I couldn't bring myself to finish the question.

'She's fading,' replied the monk. 'But she's asking for you.'

I nodded, and followed him out into the sunlight.

We walked in silence for a while, then Brother Cormac spoke. 'You should come back for more language lessons,' he said. 'I enjoyed teaching you.'

I shook my head. 'I only learned the language so I could spy on the Dalriadans,' I said. 'They'll realise that soon enough. If I were you, I wouldn't spread it about that you were the one who taught me. I wouldn't want you to get into trouble.'

'It doesn't matter why you started the lessons, Talorca,' he replied. 'I believe that our only way out of this situation is to talk it through. And given that our Dalriadan friends are notoriously bad at learning other languages, it falls to you to take that step.' He took my arm. 'You have a natural

121

ability with language, Talorca. It would be a shame to let it go to waste.' He stopped. 'Here we are,' he said. 'Before you go in, I must warn you—she doesn't look well. She may not last another day.'

I nodded, tried to ignore the sob that rose in my throat, and entered the Old Woman's house.

The house was dark, and it took my eyes a few moments to adjust. My mother sat by the Old Woman's bedside, dabbing her brow with a damp cloth. The Old Woman looked tiny and almost transparent, her hair even more wispy than usual, her face almost luminous in its paleness.

Her eyes cracked open and fixed on me.

'Talorca,' she sighed. 'Good.' She lifted one bony arm to bat away my mother's hand. 'Go, Mael,' she said. 'I need to speak to your daughter.'

My mother got up and walked out without saying a word, or even looking at me.

'Sit with me,' said the Old Woman. 'Talk with me.'

'I don't know what to say,' I said, sitting by her and taking her hand.

She chuckled, a whispering rustle in the darkness. 'Talorca at a loss for words. It had to happen some day. I'm glad I lasted long enough to see it.'

'Please don't joke,' I said.

122

'It's all a joke,' she said. 'Or none of it is.' She stared me right in the eye and I was reminded of her stronger days. 'What are we going to do about you?'

'Me? I don't matter. I'm not important. I'm worried about you, not me.'

'I didn't get up off my sick bed out of the goodness of my heart, you know,' said the Old Woman. 'I always had great plans for you, but now I've made a complete mess of them all.'

I couldn't take in what she was saying. Plans for me? What had she nearly messed up?

The Old Woman lay back and stared at the roof. 'Your mother will be the Old Woman when I'm gone,' she said.

'She can't,' I said. 'She's not like you.'

'That's probably a good thing,' said the Old Woman. 'Winter is followed eventually by summer. That's the way of things. The Winter Hag is succeeded by the Summer Queen.' She turned to look at me. 'And then you will succeed your mother in turn.'

'That's...' I didn't have words for how ridiculous that sounded. 'My mother would never let that happen. She thinks I'm...' She thought I was a horrible disappointment, but I couldn't bring myself to say it. 'Anyway, an Old Woman has to be wise, like you. I don't *think* my mother could ever be that wise, but I know *I* couldn't be.'

'Did I ever tell you the story of the rowan tree?' she asked.

That was a sudden change of topic, and I didn't know how to respond. 'Maybe. I can't remember.' She'd told me dozens of stories when I was younger, usually as rewards for doing little errands for her.

'Then let me tell you one last story,' she said. 'Once, just beyond the edge of the forest, there was a rowan tree. She was quite a lonely rowan tree, and would often look towards the forest, see all the other trees whispering to each other, and wish she could join in their conversation. But when her red berries grew on her branches, she would be visited by the birds, and their chirping made her feel less lonely, even though she couldn't understand what they said.

'One day a large magpie landed on her upper branches, making them bend alarmingly. "Be careful!" she called out, not expecting a reply, because birds and trees speak very different languages. "Oh, I'm sorry," said the magpie in his coarse voice. "I did have a message for you, but I suppose I could just leave."

'The rowan was very surprised that she could understand the magpie. "Don't leave!" she said. "Please don't leave! There's a message? For me?"

'The magpie nodded his black beak. "The Witch of

Winter has seen you brighten up the short dark days with your red berries, year after year, and would like to reward you by turning you into a wishing tree."

'The rowan had never heard of such a thing. "What's a wishing tree?" she asked.

'The magpie laughed. "It's exactly what it sounds like. People will come to you, make a wish, and you will make it come true."

'The rowan considered this. She wasn't interested in being magic, but the thought of lots of people coming to visit her made her feel excited.

'The magpie continued, "There is one rule: you can grant only good wishes. If the Witch of Winter finds that you have been granting bad wishes, she will take away your power."

'The rowan wasn't sure about this. "How can I tell a good wish from a bad wish?" she asked.

'The magpie laughed again. "That's up to you," he said, then flew away.

'The thought of lots of people coming to visit her made her feel excited, but as the weeks turned into months and the months turned into years, no-one came to visit her, and even she forgot about being a wishing tree. Then, one day at last, an old man came gathering dry sticks for firewood. He paused by the rowan, and, leaning against her trunk, said "Oh, I wish I didn't have to walk all this distance to get firewood! I wish I were rich enough to hire someone to do it for me!" At this, the rowan suddenly remembered the magpie and the Witch of Winter's gift. She concentrated hard on the old man's wish. No sooner had she thought about granting the wish than the man noticed a glint of gold out of the corner of his eye. "What's this?" he cried, delving into the long grass. "A golden brooch! I'm rich!" He jumped about like a man half his age, dancing and skipping. He had danced half-way home when he suddenly stopped, turned around, and looked at the rowan with a suspicious eye.

'The next day the old man came back, touched the trunk of the rowan, and said, in a clear voice, "I wish I would find another brooch." The rowan, pleased that the man had come back, concentrated, and with a whoop of joy the old man found another golden brooch in the grass, even finer than the first one he'd found.

'In time, word got out about the old man's sudden luck, and he told a few friends about the rowan tree. They didn't believe him at first, but when he took them to see the tree, they tried it themselves. The rowan was so happy to see so many people that she granted all the wishes—gold and silver and jewellery and fine clothes.

'Every day at least one person came to visit the rowan,

126

and she granted their wishes. She didn't feel lonely at all any more. Soon, everyone in the village grew wealthy, but for some people it wasn't enough just to have enough—they had to have more than anyone else, so the greedy people kept coming back for more and more wishes.

'One day the magpie landed on the rowan tree. "Magpie!" she called out. "Oh, I'm so happy to see you! Have you seen all the wishes I've granted? I've made so many friends!"

'The magpie shook his head and croaked at her. "The Witch of Winter is not happy with you," he said. "How many good wishes have you made, and how many bad wishes?"

'The rowan didn't know. A wish was a wish. "How do you tell a good wish from a bad one?"

'The magpie cackled. "You have just one day to work that out. If I come back tomorrow, and you haven't learned how to tell a good wish from a bad wish, the Witch of Winter will take away your powers. And your berries, too."

'The rowan was distraught. How could she tell a good wish from a bad one? All she knew was that when she granted wishes, the people kept coming back, and she didn't feel lonely. But if she couldn't work out the difference in one day, she'd lose her powers, her friends, and her berries—which would mean that even the birds wouldn't visit her any more. She'd be worse off than when she started.

'She thought and thought and thought about the wishes, but still she couldn't tell a good wish from a bad one. Day turned to night and night turned to day. The hour of the magpie's return grew closer and closer.

'Eventually, she could see the magpie flying towards her, so in desperation, the rowan concentrated. "I wish I could tell good wishes from bad wishes," she said to herself. The power of the wish flooded through her, from roots to leaf-tips.

'The magpie landed on her branches, and said, "Well?"

'The rowan quietly and confidently responded, "A selfish wish is a bad wish. And almost all wishes are selfish wishes."

'The magpie nodded. "And what makes a good wish?"

'The rowan responded, "When you wish good things for other people," she said.

'The magpie nodded again. "And what would be a good wish for yourself?"

'The rowan responded, "When you wish to be improved, rather than enriched."

'The magpie cocked his head. "What makes good wishes lead to bad wishes?"

'The rowan responded, "When you find out that your wish has come true."

'The magpie asked one last question. "How do you know all this?"

'The rowan responded, "Because I wished it."

'The magpie laughed joyously and launched itself into the air. "Then, friend rowan, you have achieved wisdom, and the Witch of Winter will let you keep your powers. Use them wisely!"

'The rowan learned from that day to use her powers sparingly. The villagers soon learned that selfish wishes for gold and silver and jewellery would no longer come true, but every once in a while a villager would have an unselfish wish, and the rowan would grant it—but in the most subtle of ways, so no-one would be able to tell whether the wish was granted or things had got better purely by chance. Over time, people stopped wishing on the tree—but they didn't stop coming to visit her. They'd come and sit beneath her branches and tell stories about how in olden times the rowan had been a magical tree that granted wishes.

'She still had her powers, and every once in a while a small child would say something like "I wish I could see a squirrel," and then would laugh when a squirrel suddenly appeared in the rowan's branches.

'And because the rowan learned wisdom, to this day, we admire it as the greatest and most magical of trees.'

The Old Woman's eyes had closed as she told the story, as if she needed to conserve her strength for speaking, but now it had finished, she opened them and looked at me. 'Do you understand the story?'

'I'm not sure,' I said. 'I don't see how it applies to me. I can't just wish myself wise.'

'Why not?' asked the Old Woman. 'The first step to becoming wise is to realise that you're not wise already. The second step is to set yourself on the path to becoming wise. The rowan could become wise with one simple wish, but she had to *want* to become wise first. It's the same with you. You've already realised that you're not wise. Your next step is to decide that you want to be better than you are. Can you do that?'

'I don't know,' I said.

'Well, I *do* know. You're going to do great things, Talorca. And one day your mother will be proud of you.'

That didn't seem likely. 'I don't know if I can do it without you.'

'You're going to have to,' she said, then closed her eyes again. 'Sit with me, Talorca. Stay with me a while. I'm so very tired.'

I squeezed her hand and sat with her into the night. A short while before dawn her grip slackened and the last breath left her body.

Chapter Nineteen
Alone

THERE WAS NO DELAY IN APPOINTING AN OLD WOMAN. A village can't exist without a matriarch, no more than the day can exist without the sun. My mother was appointed the new Old Woman within an hour of finding me clutching her predecessor's lifeless hand and sobbing quietly.

The ceremony was short and to the point. My mother stood at the clan stone and announced to the gathered crowd, monks and Dalriadans and villagers alike, that as summer became winter, she had become the Old Woman.

'I swear to provide comfort and guidance to all who need it, justice to those who deserve it, and mercy to those worthy of it,' she declaimed. 'For the common good of the village, I now dedicate my life.'

There was a muttering of approval. My mother was well-liked. The ceremony over, the words spoken, the crowd began to break up.

'Before you go,' said my mother, 'I would like to make an announcement.'

The approving muttering turned to puzzlement.

'As a symbol of the union of our communities and our peoples, I offer marriage to Nechtan mac Fergus.'

Nechtan looked as surprised as the rest of us, but recovered quickly. 'I accept your gracious offer,' he said.

'Good,' said my mother, smiling. 'Then let us have a celebration, in honour of the Old Woman who has passed, in honour of unity and union, with food and drink and music and song.'

A cheer arose from the crowd, with everyone joining in. Everyone, that is, except me.

In the noise and celebration, I slipped away and ran across the fields towards the point where the broch stood, a mixture of grief and rage churning in my gut. How could she? How could she marry the man who'd tried to have me banished? How could she replace my father so easily? My father had only been a fisherman, and not a prince, but he'd still been twice the man Nechtan mac Fergus was.

How could my mother even consider marrying someone right after the Old Woman had died? To honour the Old

Woman's memory by marrying the man she'd considered the enemy of our people was insulting. Worse than that. It was *obscene*. My feet pounded the dirt track, and before long I'd reached the broch. It was always the broch I returned to when I needed time to think. Now that my mother had betrayed me, and the Old Woman was dead, it was the only place I felt at home.

In my haste to climb the broch, I scraped my knee on the lichen-covered rocks, and blood welled in tiny droplets from the graze. I barely noticed. My fingernails chipped and broke on the stone, and I banged my elbows in the narrow passageways in the hollow walls, but eventually I climbed out onto the top of the broch.

The mid-morning light dappled the grey sea with flecks of gold that picked out the lines of the wavelets. I turned my back on the land, the village, my mother, and everyone else, and tried to stop thinking. Thinking about anything led to anger or misery.

I'd been there an hour, maybe, listening to the gulls and watching the tide come in, when the sound of falling pebbles made me aware that someone else was climbing the broch. I looked down and saw the familiar long nose of the beast, his huge eyes staring up at me, and I smiled for what felt like the first time in ages.

I was scared to open my mouth in case I sobbed. Or screamed. I could feel something, some raw, vague feeling, like a physical lump in my chest, waiting to claw its way past my throat and announce itself to the morning air.

The beast placed his head on my lap, offering me his sympathy.

I didn't want his sympathy. I didn't deserve it, not after everything I'd done. Everyone treated me as if I were a tiny child, unable to make decisions for myself.

I wished I were more like the beast.

I didn't want to live in a village with other people. I wanted nothing to do with any of them. I wished that I were a beast, a hunter, a monster, a wild creature with no family, no friends, no village. I wished that I could sever all connections with the people around me.

What was the point, after all? It always ended up in sorrow, didn't it? The Old Woman. My mother. My father. These relationships always ended up in pain of one kind or another. Wouldn't it be better to be free of all that? Free of the heartache?

'I hate them all,' I said. 'It's just you and me now, old friend.'

I rubbed the top of the beast's head, between its horns, as I'd done a dozen times before, but the beast flinched and backed away.

'What's the matter?' I asked.

The beast looked at me with his huge sea-grey eyes filled with something like understanding. I shook my head. The beast was an *animal*, not a person. A clever animal, much cleverer than a dog or a horse, but still, an animal. He couldn't actually understand what I was saying, no matter how often I tried to convince myself that he could.

But say he *did* understand. What if he didn't approve? What if, in his loneliness and solitude, the last of his kind, he heard my words and knew, deep in his bones, that I was cutting myself off from my own people? How could he approve of that?

He dipped his head in what looked like an apology and leapt from the broch. I was left staring after him as he raced into the distance, wondering how my world could have fallen apart so completely in such a short time.

Chapter Twenty
Sails

THE BROCH WASN'T A PLEASANT PLACE TO SIT. The stones were rough, and there was nowhere comfortable to rest your back. After a while, the wind chilled you down to the bone. Still, I sat there for hours, barely noticing as the sun climbed high then began to sink towards the hills in the west. I stared out to sea, but my eyes were unseeing.

Nothing lasts forever, not even misery, and by the time the western sky had turned purple I began to notice that the horrible feeling in my breast had begun to weaken. I didn't *want* it to weaken. I wanted to stay miserable and wretched and angry forever. The more I tried to keep hold of my anger, the more it slipped away, until all that was left was exhaustion and numbness.

I moved my cramped legs tentatively and started to consider climbing down the broch and making my way home. I didn't want to face my mother, but I wanted more than anything to lie on my own bed, pull a blanket over my head, and go to sleep. I stood up, my legs protesting at the movement, but as I was about to start the climb down, I caught sight of three square sails on the horizon and my heart raced. Northmen. Only Northmen used square sails. It was a group of longships heading right down the firth. Heading right for the Port.

It had to be a raiding party. The Northmen had attacked Hilltown the previous summer, killing two men and stealing several cattle, but that had been a single ship—who knew how much damage three ships full of raiders could cause?

The ships were sailing down the firth at speed. They'd be at the Port in no time at all. I had to warn my village.

I scrambled down the broch, bashing my knees and elbows against the rough stone, leaving a smeared trail of blood behind me, then raced along the track as fast as I could run. There was no time for my usual stroll to cover the distance. I pumped my legs and arms, my feet flying over the ground faster than I'd ever run before. The cold evening air burned in my lungs, and my side ached and cramped from the effort. The track dropped down into a hollow, and I lost sight of the ships.

I had to beat them to the village. I had to warn my people.

At last I reached the hill above the village, and tripped over a root or a stone or nothing at all, landing flat on my face with a thump that took all the air out of my aching lungs.

With a grunt of effort, I dragged myself to my feet and looked down into the Port.

Two longships had already run up the beach, and raiders were leaping from the hulls onto the sand, their bright weapons flashing in the evening light.

I was too late.

I watched in horror as the raiders ran up the beach. They split into two groups. The larger group headed for the monastery, while the other headed for the village. The village where my mother was.

Ignoring the pain in my legs and side, I ran towards my mother's house. Fortunately it was on the side of the village furthest from the beach, and I had a chance to get there before the Northmen.

'Mother!' I shouted as I burst through the doorway, my voice shrill and panicked. 'Mother!'

There was no sign of her. The hearth was cold and dark. I stood in complete confusion for a moment or two, my mind hammered by panic and exhaustion.

Of course. She was the Old Woman now. She'd be in the

Old Woman's house.

I ran on towards the Old Woman's house, and from up ahead I could hear screams and shouting. A sudden burst of orange fire lit the sky as the roof of Aidan's family's house burst into flames, kindled by a thrown torch. I hoped Aidan wasn't in there.

I didn't have time to check. I had to find my mother.

I rushed through the doorway of the Old Woman's house, and in the gloom saw a crouched figure holding a sword, its edge flickering in the dim light of the hearth fire's embers. With a scream I pulled my knife and launched at the Northman, stabbing wildly at his face with my little blade. He grabbed at my knife hand and fell onto his back and I fell on top of him, pushing my blade towards his face, not caring about his sword, thinking only about my mother.

'Talorca! Stop!' screamed my mother, pulling me off the man. As my vision cleared and my eyes grew used to the semi-darkness, I realised that I'd attacked Nechtan. He loosened his grip on my wrist.

'Northmen,' I said, uselessly.

'We know,' said my mother. 'Nechtan came to get me.'

'We have to go,' I said. 'It's not safe. They're burning the houses. They've already set fire to Aidan's roof.'

'Aidan? Is he all right?' asked my mother.

'I don't know,' I said. I breathed slowly, trying to calm down. 'I'm going to look for him.' I switched to the Dalriadan tongue. '*Nechtan mac Fergus, gabh cùram rium mhàthair.*' Take care of my mother.

He nodded, and picked up his sword. 'I will try,' he said. 'But nowhere is safe.'

I thought for a second. 'Take her to your hall,' I said. 'Take everyone to the hall. Gather your men.' From what I'd learned from Brother Cormac, the Northmen favoured short raids. If our people could band together in one safe place, they might be able to weather the storm.

The houses would burn. But houses can be rebuilt.

Something was nagging at my tired mind. Brother Cormac. The monks. I had to let them know to go to the hall, too.

'Talorca's right,' said my mother. 'The hall is the best place to make a stand.'

'Then go,' I said.

'You're coming with us,' said my mother. It was a statement, not a question, but I chose to interpret it differently.

'No. I have to find Aidan.'

'He's got his family to look after him, Talorca,' said my mother. 'He's not your responsibility.'

'He's my friend,' I said. So was Brother Cormac. 'I'll follow as soon as I can.' I turned to leave, and as I did I stumbled over a pile of the Old Woman's possessions, left by the doorway. My mother had obviously started to clear the house to make way for her own things. I pushed down an irrational surge of resentment at the Old Woman being swept away so quickly. Sticking out of the pile was the beast sword. I picked up the heavy blade. Something told me that a fierce Northman wasn't going to be scared by a young girl with a shellfish knife, but even a raider might think twice about rushing straight at a young woman with a sword. It was blunt, but they weren't to know that. Maybe, just maybe, it could give me a second or two in which to escape.

My mother stared at me, weighing me up in the way the Old Woman used to. She nodded to herself, as if realising that arguing with me would do no good. 'Find Aidan, then come straight after us,' she said.

'I'll see you at the hall,' I said, and left.

CHAPTER TWENTY-ONE

Pillage

AIDAN'S HOUSE WAS COMPLETELY ABLAZE. There was no way I'd be able to get to him if he was still inside. I stood for a second, the beast sword limp in my grip, trying to think what to do, when a skinny little figure was silhouetted against the light of the fire.

'Aidan!' I shouted, running up and grabbing his arm.

'Our home,' he said, gesturing vaguely at the blaze.

'Aidan,' I said firmly. 'Go to the Dalriadans' hall.'

'The hall? Why?' he said, then coughed. He seemed dazed.

'The others are there. Your parents are probably there already. You'll be safe,' I insisted, steering him in the direction of the hall.

Most of the roofs in the half of the village nearest the beach were alight, but there was no sign of the Northmen. They seemed to have headed up the hill to the monastery. They were experienced raiders. There wasn't much to steal in a village of fishermen and farmers, but a monastery? A monastery had gold and silver. And perhaps it suited the fierce gods of the Northmen to burn down the house of the monks' more gentle god.

I watched Aidan head off towards the hall long enough to make sure that he was heading in the right direction, then I turned and ran up the hill towards the monastery. I had to make sure Brother Cormac was all right.

As I passed the clan stone, I saw that a corner had been knocked off, probably from a heavy blow from an axe or club. There was no reason for it—nothing but chaos and destruction for its own sake. Did I really want to be running towards these dangerous men?

But Brother Cormac had been my friend. He'd helped save the beast. He'd taught me languages and history. I couldn't let him face the raiders alone.

The door to the vellum workshop was shattered, and I almost gagged as I looked inside. One of the monks was lying sprawled across a trough of lime, his back twisted at an unnatural angle, and his face an unrecognisable mess.

I forced myself to look again. It wasn't Brother Cormac. This monk was shorter and fatter.

I turned and emptied my stomach onto the ground. I tried to choke back a sob as I retched, and spluttered with the effort. *Good work, Talorca,* I thought. *It would be just like you to choke on your own vomit rather than be stabbed by a Northman's sword.*

I gathered myself together, wiped my mouth on my sleeve, and tried to breathe again. Where else would Brother Cormac be?

The crypt. He loved the books in the library.

As I ran towards the chapel, I saw several flaming torches cartwheel through the air and land on the building's roof. Raucous cheers filled the night. If Brother Cormac was in the chapel, he didn't have long before the whole building was alight. I gripped the beast sword more tightly and ran faster.

There was a side door to the chapel that opened right next to the hidden door to the crypt. I hoped that the Northmen had been distracted with their acts of destruction and hadn't noticed the crypt at all—there was only one entrance, after all, so if the raiders had made their way down there, any monk who'd hidden down there was certainly dead.

I pushed the image of the murdered monk from the vellum workshop out of my mind and carefully crept into the chapel. There was no sign of the Northmen—they still had to be outside, setting fire to buildings. I imagined they'd be looting the metal workshop—the monks had stores of

144

gold and silver that they used to make their sacred crosses, cups, and plates.

I pushed at the hidden door to the crypt and called out quietly. 'It's me,' I said. 'Is there anyone there?'

I crept down the stairs to see Brother Cormac kneeling in prayer at the far end of the crypt by the light of a single candle.

'Brother Cormac,' I said quietly. 'Brother Cormac,' I repeated. 'We have to go.'

'The Abbot,' said the young monk. 'He's dead.' His voice was flat and unnervingly calm.

'And we'll be dead too if we don't get out of here,' I said. I pulled at his sleeve, and a heavy book fell from his lap onto the floor. 'What's that?'

'It's the Abbot's legacy. The history of this monastery. When this place has burnt to the ground, it'll be all that's left of him.'

'Leave it,' I said. 'We need to go. Now.'

'You don't understand!' he said. 'The Abbot was like a father to me. This was the first place I could ever really call home. And now it's all gone. All gone.' I recognised the pain in his voice. It was as much self-pity as sorrow. My own voice had carried the same note more often than I cared to admit.

145

I tugged at his sleeve again.

He shook his head. 'Leave me,' he said.

I shook him by the shoulders.

'You think you're the only person who's ever lost a father?' I said. 'We've all lost people. We'll lose more today. But I'm not going to lose another friend if I can help it.' I leaned even closer and shouted in his face. 'Now get up!'

He looked confused, but the dullness seemed to leave his eyes, and he didn't resist when I pulled him to his feet. He picked up the heavy book, but I decided not to object. He needed to hold on to something; if the book was that thing, so be it.

'Come on,' I said, and pulled him towards the steps.

As we reached the foot of the stairs leading to the chapel, there was a tearing, crackling sound as one of the roof beams, weakened by the fire, cracked under its own weight and crashed down onto the crypt entrance. I leapt back as a cloud of dust and smoke billowed down the stairway, a brief rockfall of sandstone blocks in its wake.

I coughed in the dust and blinked the smoke out of my eyes. When the dust had settled, I could see that the whole stairwell had collapsed.

We were trapped.

CHAPTER TWENTY-TWO
Buried

I LOOKED ON IN HORROR FOR A MOMENT, then started to pull stones out of the stairwell. I had to jump back when I triggered another small rockfall.

'Stop,' said Brother Cormac. 'Wait a moment. It's too dangerous. I have to think.' He was starting to sound more like himself again.

'The chapel is on fire,' I said. 'We have to dig our way out. Unless you know another exit.'

'No,' said the monk. 'But if you keep pulling stones out we're going to be buried alive.'

'Buried alive or burnt to death. It's not much of a choice,' I said. I pulled at a huge piece of sandstone. It didn't budge even a tiny amount. I kicked at it, spat at it, cursed it. I picked up the beast sword and bashed at it. The heavy blade took chunks out of the block, so I bashed at it again and again, my arms aching from swinging the sword, my joints shrieking every time the blade jarred against the stone.

Chips of sandstone flew everywhere, and I spat dust from my mouth. With one enormous last crack, the block split in two. I dropped the beast sword and pulled the two halves out of the stairwell.

'Look,' I said. 'I'm getting there. We can dig our way out.'

'That was sandstone,' said the monk. 'The stone behind it is grey drystone. Much harder.'

'Then I'll have to hit it harder,' I said, and swung the beast sword with all my strength.

The blade hit the grey drystone and the shock travelled up my arm and into my skull, rattling the teeth in my head. My ears rang with the impact, loud and bright and clear, and I realised that it wasn't my ears that were ringing, but the sword. The twin blades were vibrating so quickly that their edges were blurred, and the pure clean note that came from them buried itself deep in my stomach.

The sound didn't stop. It went on and on, rising like the onset of a storm howling through a chimney-hole, insistent and terrifying. My jaw dropped, and it felt like the sound was travelling through me and out through my mouth. My whole body vibrated with the sound, the effect making my skin tingle and the hairs on my head bristle.

It seemed to go on forever, but it can only have been a few seconds. My muscles spasmed and I dropped the sword. It hit the ground with a dull clang and was silenced.

I sank to my knees.

'What was that?' asked Brother Cormac.

'The beast sword,' I said, my voice sounding quiet and harsh in comparison to the loud sweet song of the sword. 'The beast will be coming now.'

'Talorca. Are you all right?' The monk sounded worried.

'You'll see,' I said. I nodded at the stairwell. From behind the fallen stone came the sound of frantic digging.

'I'm here,' I called to the beast. 'I'm down here.'

Brother Cormac touched me on the shoulder. 'Talorca. Who is that out there?'

'I told you. The beast.'

'Who?'

'The beast. You've met him. You saved him from the arrow wound.'

The monk shook his head. 'That was just an animal,' he said.

At that, a stone rolled aside, and the beast pushed his long snout into the crypt. He growled a warning, and, barely giving us a second to take heed, he shouldered his way into the crypt. Stone scattered everywhere.

'Come on,' I said to Brother Cormac, whose mouth was hanging open. I took his hand and pushed past the beast

149

up the passageway and out into the burning church. 'This way,' I said, and pulled him past the burning beams to the door. The smoke stung our eyes and burned our lungs. We rushed out of the chapel, desperate to get clear, careless of whether any raiders waited outside for us.

I coughed, blinked smoky tears from my eyes, and scanned the area. There was no sign of the Northmen.

'We have to get away from here,' I said, as the beast rolled on the grass to extinguish sparks that smouldered on his short fur. 'We have to go to the hall. That's where everyone else is gathering.' I ran off down the hill, glancing back to make sure that the monk and the beast were following close behind. I couldn't see any of the other monks. I hoped they'd been able to get away. The light from the burning buildings cast an orange glow over everything, and the stink of smoke filled the air. The whole monastery was ablaze—every roof alight, every door smashed in.

We ran on down the hill, the beast keeping pace easily with me, Brother Cormac struggling with his heavy book.

A silhouetted figure leapt out in front of us, a bow in his hands, an arrow ready and drawn and pointing right at my head. I came to a sudden stop. The beast growled and made ready to leap, but before he could move, the archer loosed his arrow. It flew past my head so close that I could feel the wind of its passing, and a gurgling scream came from behind me.

I turned to see a Northman, his axe raised, stop in his tracks and with his free hand claw at the arrow buried deep in his throat. He'd been seconds from reaching us.

Finn set up another arrow and stepped forward. He aimed and shot again, this time right into the Northman's heart. The big man keeled over and breathed no more.

'What are you doing here?' I asked.

'My father sent me to find you,' said Finn.

'You've found me now,' I said. 'Let's go. To the hall.' I ran off before Finn could ask any questions about the beast. As we neared the bottom of the hill, I could see the two longships on the beach, and something nagged at the back of my mind.

Before I could work out what was bothering me, the beast howled, and we swung around to see a mob of ten or twelve Northmen bearing down on us. They dropped their loot—gold and silver cups and plates—raised their weapons, and charged with a deep horrible battle-scream that turned my blood to ice.

The beast howled again, howling like a dozen wolves all at once, and the Northmen hesitated, but only for a second. I lifted the beast sword, for all the good it would do me, and

Finn raised his bow. Brother Cormac made the sign of the cross.

One Northman, his beard long and intricately braided, a bear-hide draped around his shoulders, raced far ahead of his companions, a horrific scream erupting from his throat, an axe in each hand, their blades broad and deadly. Finn fired an arrow right into his chest and he didn't break stride.

The beast moved in front of me, crouching ready to leap and growling. Behind me I could hear Brother Cormac praying in Latin. I didn't think it would do any good.

Finn shot another arrow, but this one went off to the side. I'd didn't think he'd have time to draw again before the warrior was on top of us. The big Northman threw one axe—it went past me and I heard a grunt as Brother Cormac fell to the ground.

This was it. The end. I shifted my grip on the beast sword and waited for my fate.

The Northman raised his remaining axe, but a spear flew through the air and stabbed deep into the warrior's thigh. He stumbled, fell to one knee, but as he started to rise again, another spear hit him in the chest.

Finn shot an arrow into the warrior's gut, and it was joined by a hail of more arrows. I looked around, and saw the most glorious sight I'd ever seen. The whole village was running up the hill, with Nechtan and his men leading the way with their spears and bows, followed closely by the rest of the village. My mother had a spear in her hands. Even Aidan had joined in, waving a shellfish knife above his head so vigorously that I feared for the safety of his ears.

Another volley of arrows followed the first, this time aimed at the rest of the Northmen. The arrows fell short, but their leader, a broad-chested warrior with a golden helmet, shouted a command, and the Northmen turned and ran for their longships, pausing only to snatch up some of the loot they'd dropped.

The beast relaxed, the bristling hair on the back of his neck flattening, and I laid my hand on the back of his head.

'Talorca!' cried my mother. 'Talorca! Are you all right?'

'I'm fine,' I said, and I realised that it was true. It was over. We'd survived the raid. We'd lost people, we'd lost gold and silver, and we'd lost buildings, but the community was unharmed. We'd all—no, wait. The Abbott was dead and…

'Brother Cormac!' I said. The monk was lying on the ground, the Northman's axe in his chest. He groaned, then sat up, and I could see the axe *wasn't* in his chest, but embedded deep in his heavy book.

'My history,' he said mournfully, pulling the axe out of the book. I grinned. It was typical of the monk to be more worried about the condition of his book than his own hide.

I looked at Nechtan and his men.

'Nechtan mac Fergus, you have my thanks,' I said.

'And you have mine,' he responded. 'You thought clearly in a crisis. I thought only to protect your mother, but you thought to bring us all together at the hall. It was a good plan. Together, we are strong.'

He looked down towards the sea. The Northmen had pushed their longships back into the sea and were already sailing back across the firth. Both ships would soon be out of sight.

Wait.

Both ships?

But there had been three ships sailing down the firth. Where was the third?

CHAPTER TWENTY-THREE

The Third Ship

NECHTAN SHOWED NO SIGN OF STOPPING HIS SPEECH about unity and strength. 'There's a third ship,' I said, interrupting him.

'What?' asked my mother.

'There were three ships coming down the firth. If two ended up here, then the third...'

'Must have landed further up the coast,' said Brother Cormac.

'The cattle. They're after the cattle,' I said.

'If they take the cattle...' said my mother.

'We'll starve this winter,' I completed her thought.

We stood in silence for a moment or two, our victory over the Northmen forgotten. We faced starvation. The survival of the community was at stake. Some of us would die. I looked at Aidan—he was so small and skinny; he might not last a winter of starvation. Others would join him, and still more would leave in search of better fortune elsewhere.

It could be the end of the Port.

'I won't let it happen,' I said.

'It's too late,' said my mother.

'Not yet, it's not,' I said. 'Keep this safe,' I said, handing Brother Cormac the beast sword. I placed my hand on the beast's shoulder. 'Are you ready for another run?' I asked.

The beast grunted, and the villagers gasped. With the gloom and the fire and the Northmen, the grey-furred beast by my side had managed to avoid their attention. When he growled, they couldn't avoid noticing him any more.

'Let's go,' I said, and the beast bowed his head exactly as he'd done before, letting me climb onto his back before lowering his horns over my thighs to lock me in place more securely than any saddle. Before my mother or Nechtan or anyone could say anything, the beast shot off up the coast, his powerful legs pounding the grass, his curled claws kicking up dirt in great lumps behind us.

I bent down, flattening myself against his neck to avoid being pulled off by the wind.

'There it is,' I said, as we raced along the cliff-top. The third ship was sitting on the beach, gangplanks propped against its hull to form a ramp for the cattle as the Northmen herded them down across the sands.

'Come on,' I urged. 'We don't have much time!'

We raced down the cliff path and across the rocks—the Northmen had nearly reached their longship with the cattle, and we didn't have time to spare. The great hairy horned beasts were difficult to herd, as I knew all too well from experience, and it didn't look like the Northmen were particularly good cattlemen, but it would only be a matter of minutes before they were all on board the longship.

'I've got an idea,' I said to the beast, my mouth pressed close to his ear. 'Remember when you distracted the Dalriadans so I could burn their hall? You imitated a wolf? Do you think you could do that again?' I didn't know if he understood, so I sucked in a breath of air and howled. 'Arrooooooo!'

It was perhaps the most unconvincing wolf howl anyone has ever performed, and the cattle certainly weren't fooled, but it gave the beast the idea.

He opened his jaws and howled.

The noise was deafening. The howl echoed from the cliffs and seemed to double in volume, until soon it sounded like an entire pack of wolves was bearing down on the beach.

The cattle twitched their horned heads, looking around to see where the threat was coming from. They snorted and bellowed in panic, their hairy hooves snatching at the sand as they tried to decide which way to run.

The Northmen with their long spears shouted and prodded, and for a second it seemed like they'd manage to regain control and direct the cows back towards their ship.

But then we were upon them, the beast's jaws snapping at the cows' hindquarters, and the fold of cattle exploded in all directions.

One Northman was tossed up into the air by a casual flick of a cow's horns, while another was shouldered aside.

'*Ulfr!*' shouted a Northman seeing us amongst the cattle, which I knew from Brother Cormac's lessons meant 'wolf'. The raider raised his axe, threw it with a blur of his arm, and I felt the wind as it passed a hair's-breadth from my head.

The cattle had scattered, terrified of the beast and his wolf-like howling. The Northmen would have no chance to steal them now.

'Let's get out of here,' I urged the beast, but he was lost in a frenzy. He leapt straight at one of the Northmen, claws outstretched, and only the warrior's quick reflexes in raising his shield saved him from being slashed to pieces. The shield splintered, and the Northman was knocked to the ground.

'Come *on!*' I shouted, digging my knees into his flanks as I'd seen horsemen do. He growled but reluctantly allowed me to direct him down the beach back towards to the Port.

I looked back over my shoulder. The Northmen were gathering up their wounded and pushing their longship back into the firth.

We'd done it. We'd driven them off, and saved the cattle.

As we reached the harbour of the Port, I became aware of a disturbance on the beach. It looked like one of the Northmen had been left behind, and he was hunkered down behind a huge driftwood tree on the seaweed line, holding off the villagers with a small armoury of bow and arrows, several spears, and an axe.

The villagers were crowded amongst the dunes. They had the higher ground, the longer range, and the Northman was outnumbered, but still, I didn't like it. I was worried for my people. They would win, almost certainly, but at what cost? The Northmen were fierce raiders, used to fighting and killing, and with the exception of a few Dalriadans, my people were farmers and fishermen and monks. Some would certainly die.

I couldn't let it happen.

I rushed up the beach towards my people, the beast cantering at my side.

'*Fuirich!*' I called out to Nechtan. 'Wait!' I stopped, out of breath.

'We cannot stop,' said Nechtan. 'Death awaits the raiders who stole from us. It is justice.'

'If you attack him, some of us will die,' I said. 'There is another way. Tell them, Brother Cormac.'

'Me?' said the monk, surprised. He was still fretting over the torn pages of his book. I gestured and he came forwards through the crowd.

'You've read the stories of the Northmen. You've known hostages from the Earls. Battles don't have to end with everybody dead, do they?'

'Well, no,' said Brother Cormac.

'Then talk to them,' I said.

'I barely know any words of their language,' protested the monk.

'You have to *try*,' I said. 'Use their stories. Their poetry.'

Brother Cormac looked unconvinced.

'I'll come with you,' I said.

The beast growled, quietly enough that only the monk and I could hear, and stepped forward. He was coming too.

'I won't allow it,' said my mother, pushing her way to the front.

'It's the only way,' I said. 'There's been enough death

160

today, don't you think?'

'But...' she began. I shook my head.

'It's the only way,' I repeated. I looked up at the monk. 'Come on.' I turned my back on my mother and walked towards the longship, my hands held out to the sides, palms open and obviously empty of weapons.

The Northman popped his head above the tree trunk and lifted a spear.

The beast roared, and the Northman ducked back down.

As we drew closer, Brother Cormac found his courage and stepped in front of me. He lifted his head, drew a breath, and spoke.

I don't know exactly what he said. I caught words like 'ravens' and 'blood' and 'enough'. The way he was speaking, rhythmic and sing-song, suggested that he was reciting from their poetry.

But the gist of what he said was this: 'Lay down your weapons. There has been enough death today—the ravens have had their fill of blood. Surrender and you will be taken to the King's court as a hostage, where you will be treated well, and may be traded back to your own people in time.'

For a long, long minute, there was silence from the Northman. At last, he stood up, a vicious-looking spear in his hand. He looked at the beast, the horned wolf-monster by my side. If Brother Cormac's words couldn't convince him, maybe the presence of the beast would.

I held my breath as he lifted the spear, and let it out with a sigh of relief as he tossed the weapon into the sand in front of him. The Northman nodded, and uttered a single throaty syllable:

'*Ja.*'

Brother Cormac turned to me, a huge smile on his face.

'He says yes,' said the monk.

I'd worked that out for myself.

CHAPTER TWENTY-FOUR

On the Watchtower

THE GREAT HALL RANG WITH LAUGHTER AND MUSIC, and the smoky smell of roasting meat mingled with the fresh-baked scent of honey cakes and wafted throughout the chamber. Winter was on us, but the village was fighting back against the cold and darkness by filling the hall with warmth and light. It turned out winter customs weren't so different amongst our people and the Dalriadans—story-telling, music, feasting, and dancing.

I wasn't so keen on the dancing, but Diarmuid—Finn's youngest brother—had insisted, and was whirling me around until I felt a bit dizzy.

'All right, all right, that's enough for now,' I said.

The boy nodded, his cheeks flushed. 'See you later,' he said, and ran off to join his brother Conan, who was sitting in a corner playing knucklebones with Aidan.

Aidan had become good friends with Conan and Diarmuid, but if I'd thought that would let me off the hook,

163

I'd been mistaken. Sometimes I longed for the days when I only had *one* pretend brother following me around. These days I had four not-quite-brothers, and that was a bit too much for anyone. Would it have been so much to ask for just *one* sister amongst that lot?

But still, I couldn't complain. Since the Northmen's raid, I'd been making an effort to feel a new appreciation for my community, with all its different members. I'd even almost come to an understanding with my mother. I still thought her marriage to Nechtan was a mistake, but I didn't quite see it as the betrayal of my father's memory that I once had. My mother had tried to explain herself to me, but I didn't really understand. She'd said that she had married once for herself, and once for the village. That didn't seem to ring entirely true when I saw her laughing and joking with her new husband, but still, it meant Nechtan wasn't a replacement for my father, but something—someone—different. I still didn't like the man, but I'd almost come to accept his presence in my village, my home, and my life.

'Leaving so soon, Talorca?' asked my mother. She'd noticed me drifting towards the door.

I nodded. 'I told Finn I'd take over the look-out at the broch.'

She brushed a loose hair away from my face and tucked

it behind my ear. 'I understand. You don't like these gatherings very much, do you?'

I shrugged. 'They're all right.'

She tilted her head and looked at me. 'But sometimes you prefer to be alone?'

I nodded.

'I understand,' she said. 'You know, after all that happened this summer—'

'That's all over,' I said. I didn't want to be reminded of all the stupid things I'd done. I couldn't face another lecture.

'I know. It was a difficult time for all of us. But I just wanted to say—I'm proud of you. I'm proud of how you're growing up.' She gave me a quick hug. 'Now, you'd better hurry, or Finn will be grumpy.'

Outside the hall, the sudden cold bit into my skin, and I wrapped my winter cloak around my shoulders. I didn't know what to think about what my mother had said. I'd expected a telling-off, but instead...

I pushed it to the back of my mind, huddled down into my cloak, and set off along the path. The winter breeze cleared the smoky smells from my head. It was going to be even colder up on the watchtower, and for a moment I considered heading back to the village to pick up another fleece. But no. Finn was waiting for me, and, while we hadn't become friends in the months since my mother and his father had married, we'd settled for putting up with each other in a way that seemed right for a not-quite-brother-and-sister. Still, I didn't want to make him any grumpier than usual, and the one thing he couldn't stand was when I turned up late for my watch.

'Finn!' I called from the base of the broch.

He peeked over the edge. 'About time, too,' he said. 'You should have been here ages ago, Sea Hag.'

'I'm right on time,' I countered. He still sometimes called me 'Sea Hag' but the spite had drained out of the nickname. Mostly. 'It's still an hour until sunset.'

He grunted something jumbled and disappeared from sight. At length, he emerged from the shadow at the base of the broch. As usual, I could climb up or down the broch far more quickly than he could.

'I'm off,' he said.

'If you hurry to the Great Hall, there might be some roast meat and cakes left. If Diarmuid and Conan haven't eaten them all.'

He mumbled and headed back into the village. There would be plenty of food. The celebrations would continue

166

long into the night, but I was happy to be on look-out duty.

I climbed the broch, and when I reached the top, I scanned the seas on all sides. We hadn't had any more attacks from the Northmen, but I'd insisted that we use the broch as a watchtower to keep an eye on the firths, just in case. We all took turns, so no-one had to spend too many hours up on the cold broch, but I liked it up there, so I often volunteered to take other people's shifts in exchange for small favours.

It was nice to be alone.

Well, mostly alone.

The beast yawned, stretched, and climbed up onto the top of the broch with me. His tail flicked some rocks and lichen off his fur. He'd been sleeping curled up in the rubble at the base of the broch.

'You like to stay hidden when Finn's on watch, don't you?' I said. 'I don't blame you.'

The beast stared out to sea. The people of the village had come to terms with the existence of a strange beast mostly by pretending that he didn't exist. They avoided the broch as much as possible, except when they had to stand watch like Finn, and the beast helped by staying hidden from view. That meant he was always happy when I turned up and he could come out into the open. I was glad. My secret friend was no longer a secret, but for the most part I still had the beast to myself.

'There was a nice sea trout in my nets today,' I said. 'I thought you'd like it.' I pulled the fish out of my bag and the beast wolfed it down.

The beast sighed and stretched out on the broch.

'You're getting fat and lazy,' I said.

I thought back to all the times the beast and I had played tricks on the Dalriadans. I still wasn't completely happy about them living in our village, but I was starting to think that all my reasons for hating the Dalriadans didn't matter so much, now we needed help against our common enemy.

But our people had started down a path of unity with the Dalriadans that wasn't entirely equal. They still had difficulty learning our language, while we found it much easier to learn theirs.

That was the way it was, unfortunately. Their language was already becoming the language of our kings and noblemen even before Nechtan and his men came here.

It's a terrible thing for a language to die, though, and I wondered whether, if we didn't take care, that might happen to our tongue. Eventually, there would be only one person left who spoke the language, and that... that would be the loneliest feeling in the world.

'You know all about that, don't you?' I said to the beast. 'I wonder, was there ever a beast tongue that you used with your kin? Was there ever a day when you became the last of your kind, the last to know your language? What's it like to be last and alone?'

He looked up at me, and I felt as if I could see the thoughts and understanding flickering behind his eyes. He put his head on my lap, heavy and warm.

I sighed. 'Don't worry, my friend. We'll always have each other.' I rubbed the soft fur of his head. He closed his eyes contentedly, a deep rumbling coming from his chest, and began to snore.

'You might be last, but you're not alone.'

THE END

Author's Note

I've always been fascinated by the Pictish Beast. The Picts left behind very little of their culture, with the exception of the amazing carved stones you can find across Scotland, and while most of the animals on those stones are recognisably snakes, wolves, eagles, salmon, and so on, two-fifths of the creatures carved on the stones are images of the enigmatic 'beast'. What was it? It must have been important, to be so common. Was it a dolphin, with its long nose? But dolphins don't have horns or legs. A kelpie? We'll probably never know. But it's these mysteries and gaps in history that fire the imagination, so when I came to write this story about Pictish times, I couldn't help it.

It had to be about the beast.

Glossary of Gaelic Phrases and Pronunciation Guide

Approximate pronunciations are given inside slash marks. The 'ch' should be pronounced /*ch*/ as in 'loch'.

Chapter 4 – Arrival

Ciamar a tha sibhse? – How are you? (formal; plural) /*kimar a ha sheev-shi*/

Tha sinn gu math – We are well /*ha shin goo ma*/

Tapadh leat – Thank you /*tapa lat*/

Feumaidh mi a bhruidhinn ris am maighstir na baile mu dheidhinn nan stuthan cudromach – I need to speak to the master of the village about important matters /*fame-ee mee a vree-in reesh am myshter na balla moo yane nan stoohan coodrimoch*/

'S e cailleach uisge a th'ann – It's the sea hag /*shay kigh-lach oosh-gi a ha-oon*/

Càit a bheil do phiorbhaig-feamad? – Where is your wig of seaweed? /*caatch a vell doh fear-a-vag fe-mid*/

Chapter 6 – The Hunt

Mac-tìre! – Wolf! /*mac-teer*/

Chapter 11 – A Dinner Party

Chan eil innte ach trioblaid – She's nothing but trouble / *han yell een-chi ach trooblich/*

Tha i ag ithe mar 's gur e rabaid a th' innte – She's eating as if she was a rabbit /*ha ee ageech-e mar sgoor e rabbitch a heen-chi/*

Chapter 13 – The Coracle Thief

Thalla dhan gharadh agus faigh an curach – Go to the cave and get the coracle /*halla yan yar-i agus figh an coorach/*

Chapter 17 – The Trial

Chan eil feum aig duine sam bith a bhith a' bruidhinn a' chànain agam – There is no need for anyone to speak my language /*han yell fame aig doon-yi sam-bee a-vee a-bree-in ach-hanning agum/*

Chapter 20 – Sails

Gabh cùram rium mhàthair – Look after my mother
/gav cooram rowm vahir/

Chapter 23 – The Third Ship

Fuirich! – Wait! */foorich/*

Would you like to learn more Gaelic?
Visit http://learngaelic.net/

Acknowledgements

The Beast on the Broch is set in Portmahomack on the Tarbat Ness peninsula in north-east Scotland, where I lived with my Mum Elizabeth, Dad Robert, and brother Alan in the late 70s and early 80s. We lived right at the tip of the peninsula, where I've set the broch of the title; but it was a different type of tower in those days: a lighthouse. It was the conversations I had with my Dad about our old lighthouse home, and its long history with Picts and Vikings, that led me to the idea for this story. The story about the wishing tree that the Old Woman tells is based on a story my Dad wrote for me and Alan over 40 years ago, too. Without my Dad, this book could never have existed. Unfortunately, he never got the chance to read it, but I like to think he'd have enjoyed it.

Martin Carver's book *Portmahomack: Monastery of the Picts* provided me with a whole host of archaeological information about the monastery at Portmahomack and its likely fate at the swords of the Vikings. None of this was known when I lived at Tarbat Ness; history is not static, and our understanding of our past increases all the time. Needless to say, all historical errors and fancies are mine alone.

The pictishstones.org.uk website is a treasure trove of facts and pictures about Pictish times, including the images used for chapter headings and the illustration of the clan stone in this book. (The pictures are used under terms of the Open Government Licence.)

My friend and colleague Colin Jones provided a daily dose of encouragement and commiseration as we fought our way towards the goal of publication. A difficult journey is always made easier with a travelling companion.

Thanks to Anne and Helen at Cranachan for believing in this story, for understanding what I was trying to do, and for helping to make it as good as it can be. Thanks also to Lauren for providing the Gaelic used in this book; what little Gaelic I used to know is long forgotten.

Cover artist Dawn Treacher really brought Talorca and the beast to life. I couldn't have hoped for a better cover, and I think it's absolutely beautiful.

Like many new writers, I depend on Twitter for a support group. Thanks especially to #ClanCranachan writers Helen MacKinven, Barbara Henderson, and Michelle Sloan; my old Dundee competition friends Lindsay Littleson and Joe Lamb; Abi Elphinstone for agreeing to provide a cover quote; and Jeremy de Quidt for his well-timed encouragement right when I needed it.

And as always, most of all, thanks go to my partner Sandra, who read the rough first version of this book and saw its faults; but more importantly saw its potential. If this book succeeds in what I set out to do, it's thanks to Sandra's keen eye, patience, support, and understanding.

About the Author

John K Fulton is the son of a lighthouse keeper, and grew up all around the coast of Scotland. These remote and lonely locations instilled in him a life-long love of books and the sea. He studied at the universities of St. Andrews and Dundee, and now lives in Leicester with his partner Sandra. While Leicester is about as far from the sea as you can get in the UK, their home is stuffed with books, which is the next-best thing.

His first book, the WWI spy thriller *The Wreck of the Argyll*, won the Great War Dundee Children's Book Prize.

You can contact John at www.johnkfulton.com, on Twitter @johnkfulton, or as johnkfulton on Instagram.

yesteryear

Also available in the Yesteryear Series

The Revenge of Tirpitz
by M. L. Sloan
The thrilling WW2 story of a boy's role in the sinking of the warship *Tirpitz*.

Fir for Luck
by Barbara Henderson
The heart-wrenching tale of a girl's courage to save her village from the Highland Clearances.

To download free reading resources and lesson plans to accompany all of our books please visit:

www.cranachanpublishing.co.uk

pokey hat

Thank You for Reading

As we say at Cranachan,
'the proof of the pudding is in the reading'
and we hope that you enjoyed *The Beast on the Broch.*

Please tell all your friends and tweet us with your
#thebeastonthebroch feedback, or better still, write an
online review to help spread the word!

We only publish books which excite and inspire us, so if
you'd like to experience other unique and
thought-provoking books, please visit our website:

cranachanpublishing.co.uk

and follow us
@cranachanbooks
for news of our forthcoming titles.

cranachan

Lightning Source UK Ltd.
Milton Keynes UK
UKOW06f0151300816

281774UK00004B/24/P